Dickens Holiday Of Lights

By

Judy Kentrus

Dickens Holiday of Lights

Dickens Holiday Romance

Author: Judy Kentrus

www.judykentrus.com

Book Title: Dickens Holiday of Lights

Edited by: Joyce Lamb Editing

Dickens Holiday of Lights

Chapter 1

Elise twirled the scraper spatula atop the batter on the griddle, ensuring the crepe's thickness was perfectly even. As soon as it was a golden brown, she expertly folded the pastry into a triangle and placed it on her daughter's breakfast plate.

Sophie cut it into bite-size pieces. Elise cringed when her daughter drenched them in maple syrup.

"Mom, you make the best crepes. I love the real syrup we get from Mr. Maple's farm, not that fake kind in the store."

Elise glanced at her fourteen-year-old son sitting across the table. His plate of three crepes had gone untouched. Normally, the kids weren't allowed to use their tablets or phones while eating, but Emile was working on a special project for his art class, so she'd given him a pass this time.

"How close are you to finishing your report?"

Emile lifted his eyes away from the screen. "I have to do a little more research, but I'll finish it by tomorrow and turn it in on Monday."

"Great. Now eat while the crepes are relatively warm."

Emile shoved a bite into his mouth, chewed, and swallowed. "Mom, why do we have singing pipes in this house? The wood doors and floors creak, too."

"When I turn the hot water on in the upstairs bathroom, the pipes knock and whistle," Sophie added.

Elise was always amazed at how quickly they could jump from one subject to another, specifically their noisy house. Elise set her plate on the table and sprinkled fresh berries and powdered sugar on her crepe.

"Are you kidding me? The house may be old, but it's uniquely musical! The previous owner told the realtor the stones were brought from a quarry in Pennsylvania. When tapped, the stones give off special sounds. He called it the Ringing Rocks House."

Emile curled his lip. "Mom, really."

She held up a hand like she was taking an oath. "Honest." She sighed. "It's not the modern house that we lived in Chicago, but it fit my house-purchasing budget."

Their lives had been turned upside down this past year, but she was lucky to have two beautiful children. They shared their late father's leaf-green eyes. Emile also had his father's russet hair. He habitually brushed the longer hair off his forehead. He had the height of an average fourteen-year-old and favored jeans and sweatshirts with graphic prints.

Sophie's light brown hair had natural red highlights. She liked wearing it in pigtails since it allowed everyone to see her newly pierced ears. Her favorite color was light blue, so many of her tops featured some form of blue, which she wore with jeans or leggings.

This question needed to be asked. "Both of you, look at me. I know it was hard for you to give up your friends and move to a new place, but do you like living in Dickens?"

Sophie jabbed her fork into the last piece of crepe on her plate. "At first, it was hard, but I have a lot of new friends. Lynnie, Holly, and Ivy are my besties." Her eyes flared wide. "We're using Lynnie's baby brother to practice for when we become babysitters!"

"Practice? What do you mean? Where is Mrs. Nielson when you're playing adventures in babysitting?"

"Oh, she's right there. Lynnie showed us how to put a diaper on him. He just started walking, so we help him." Sophie made a yucky face. "He doesn't like green beans and spits them out! Ew!"

"You've made new friends and are learning babysitting skills. Is there anything else that makes you happy that we're living in Dickens?"

"I like that we live close to Aunt Britta and Uncle Dane and visit them at 2 Sisters Kringle and Fudge. They let me help make fudge. I'm going to try out for *The Bells of St. Dickens* play at the old library on Christmas Eve. Lynnie said we'll be on cable television!"

"This year, it will be at the event center so that we can accommodate more people. So, you're good with living in a musical house and like living in Dickens?"

"Yeah, it's good." Sophie picked up her plate and set it on the scarred Formica counter. "I need to change before we leave for the library."

"But you're already dressed."

"I forgot. We're reading *A Boy Called Christmas* for our book club, so Lynnie, me, Holly, and Ivy decided to wear Christmas shirts."

"Wait, before you run off. Where's the cat?"

"Simone is sleeping on my bed. She was cold, so I wrapped her in a blanket with her favorite toy mouse."

Elise didn't want to remind her nine-year-old daughter, who had a very kind heart, that their rescue tabby had been living in an unheated basement when they moved in.

Elise ate half of her crepe and drank some of her herbal tea. "Your turn," she said to Emile.

He leaned back in his chair. "If I tell you the truth, it will make you feel bad."

She thought she already knew, but she needed him to express his feelings. "I asked, so be honest with me."

"The kids think I'm weird."

Apparently, she was wrong. This was the first she'd heard of this. "Weird?"

"Yeah, because I like art—you know, paintings by famous people. When we lived in Chicago, we went to museums and art galleries. I like looking at all kinds of art, not just Van Gogh or Monet."

She wanted to hold him and absorb his disappointment, wishing there had been some other way. She didn't dare share the real reason they'd had to move here, which still gave her nightmares.

"Emile, I wish we could have stayed in Chicago, but I had to do what was best for you, your sister, and me. The job offer I got here in Dickens and being able to live close to your Aunt Britta and Uncle Dane is what we needed. I know you miss your father. I miss him, too. He'll always be alive in our hearts and memories."

"I know," he said without looking her in the face.

"Your aunt and uncle are so happy we live close to them. Thanksgiving was special this year since they were able to join us. You're an A-plus student in school."

He continued to avoid looking her in the face, giving her the impression he was holding back more.

"So, what else is bothering you?"

He moved away from the table to go into the small closet where they stored their backpacks when they came in from school. He pulled out a flyer.

"The art teacher handed this out the other day, but I didn't show it to you. They're starting an art club after school, to meet two days a week. I didn't say anything because you work late the same days as the art club. I'd have no way to get home from school."

She read over the flyer that outlined the club's intention. "I think this is wonderful. Things have slowed down at the event center, and I'll be working from home more." She held out a hand. "Give me a pen, and I'll sign the permission form for you to join the club."

He threw his arms around her neck. "You're the best mom! I'll keep an eye on Sophie at the library if their book club meeting ends before you come to pick us up after your meeting at the event center."

"I take it you're going to do research on your art project?"

"Hailey and I agreed to meet in the research room."

Elise fought hard not to smile. He'd shared very little about his girlfriend. "Is she into art, too?"

He blushed slightly. "Yeah, graphic arts and she's really good. She's joining the art club, too."

"Have you shared any of your wonderful graphic figures with the kids who call you weird?"

"Hailey loves them, but I haven't shown the others. They'll laugh at me."

She dipped her head to the side. "Personally, I think they'd be surprised at some of your unique characters. Casually mention that you're creating a league of superheroes for a graphic novel and that the characters are based on your friends. They'll try to figure out who you selected."

"Mom, you're really smart." He grinned, revealing a full set of braces.

Elise paused. "I've been toying with the idea of having a logo done for the event center. Do you know of anyone who could create something unique? Maybe ask a friend for help."

The smile she loved was back. "Mom, that's a great idea." He put his empty plate on the counter and grabbed his tablet from the table. "I'm going to call Hailey right now, and then I have to take a shower."

She sat at the table and sipped her herbal tea. *Crisis averted.*

She still had an hour before she had to drop the kids off at the library annex. From there, she had a meeting with Sebastian Nielson and Axel Frost, the owners of the Dickens Event Center and Train Museum. This would be the first Christmas for the event center and the train museum.

She'd taken on a lot of responsibility, helping to make Sebastian and Axel's dream come true. They'd refused to let a few narrow-minded individuals who opposed the center during its planning stages ruin their plans. It hadn't cost the small-town government a cent. Axel had the financial means to cover the cost of refurbishing a bank barn built by German immigrants in 1840.

She knew about dreams, but she'd learned the hard way that making wishes on stars, finding that pot of gold at the end of a rainbow, discovering a four-leaf clover, or crossing your fingers never worked.

The knocking, followed by a slow, easy whistle, let her know Emile was taking his shower. The pipes' musical effects varied. At times, she laughed and stepped into the mind of a composer writing a song.

She loved the kitchen's warm, cozy feel. The old plaster walls were painted a soft cream color. The wood floors weren't completely level, but they were clean and polished. The kids were shocked when they realized there wasn't a dishwasher. She'd added a short red-and-white-gingham curtain across the top half of the square-pane windows above the sink. It matched the tablecloth and chair cushions. The chipped white enamel on the old stove gave it personality.

In the corner, there was a potbelly stove and a soft-cushioned wingback chair. On cold nights, she loved to sit there and relax with a cup of tea, absorbing the warmth from the fire.

She clasped the gold fleur-de-lis pendant on a chain around her neck, a cherished gift from her late grandmother. "Claude," she said to her late husband, "you left a mess, but I'm doing my best. The children and I have made a new life with new friends, and we're happy. The shyster money lender you borrowed money from hasn't found us. Hopefully, he never will."

Feeling-sorry-for-herself time was over. She stepped up to the old enamel sink and added liquid soap to a large basin. She'd just turned on the warm water when Sophie rushed into the kitchen.

"Mom, can we go to 2 Sisters Kringle and Fudge after the library? They have a new flavor with…" She stopped, and her eyes widened when she saw the mound of bubbles. "Mom! Let's do it!"

Sophie's giddiness was infectious. Why not? "Only if you'll help me wipe up the floor!"

"Deal!"

"Hold out your hands." Elise scooped up a mountain of soap bubbles. "Some for you and some for me. Now blow."

Their warm breaths sent mounds of bubbles into the air as they sang, "I'm forever blowing bubbles, pretty bubbles in the air. They fly so high, nearly reaching the sky…"

Elise continued the rest in her head. *Then, like dreams, they fade and die…*

~ 12 ~

A little after eleven o'clock, Elise, Emile, and Sophie arrived at the Dickens Library Annex. A dozen cars occupied the plowed parking lot. Elise was more than happy with the six inches of snow on the ground. Having lived in Chicago, she was used to snow showers and squalls of lake-effect snow off Lake Michigan.

When visitors entered the former church, they were greeted by a ten-foot-tall artificial tree that had been put up two weeks ago. Lace figurines, ribbons, glass angels, bows, and electric candles created a Victorian theme.

Sunlight pierced the clear, lead-paned, arched windows, bringing natural light into the room. The stone floors of the Puritan-style church were original and had been well-tended.

She breathed in the scent of aged tomes on the rows of wooden bookshelves. A card catalog was housed in small wooden drawers in their original framing.

Sophie spotted Lynnie, Holly, and Ivy and immediately took off to join them. Elise had to chuckle when all four girls then headed for the ladies' room.

Emile mumbled, "See you later," and walked in the direction of the reference room.

Elise found Karla arranging the folding chairs in the children's section. She'd dressed for the season—black leggings and a red sweater with a silk-screened picture on it with the words Christmas Is Coming.

"Morning, Karla. When we walked in, Sophie encountered Lynnie, Holly, and Ivy, and they all ran to the bathroom."

"I don't get it." Karla shook her head. "We both live a short distance from the library, and the girls have to go to the bathroom as soon as they get here." She placed the book the book club was going to read on the chair positioned at the head of the horseshoe arrangement.

"The four of them spell trouble—in a mischievous way. Emile headed to the reference room and knows he must take care of his sister if my meeting with your husband and Axel exceeds your reading time. You have my cell number if there's a problem."

Karla looked around to make sure they were alone, then spoke in a lowered voice. "Your suggestion is fabulous. Dickens Holiday of Lights will generate so much interest for the event center. Using the Dickens Depot Railroad Station as a children's party venue is another great idea."

"How much static from the powers that be are we going to get? I know about the resistance you got when you purchased the old bank barn."

Karla pursed her lips. "My sister, Freja, can give you an earful. That's why we're keeping this quiet until all of our plans are in place. I love the idea that the downtown flavor is changing with the opening of a restaurant specializing in crepes. I thought they were only eaten for breakfast."

"Once again, the public is misinformed, but I don't have time to tell you about the fabulous cuisine my husband, Claude, and I prepared when we worked at a small bistro in Chicago."

Elise blinked rapidly to erase the teary film from her eyes. They'd been so close to realizing their dream of opening their own creperie, and then he was killed in a car accident. The police had let her know that the accident had been declared a DUI, based on the number of empty wine bottles in the back seat. That determination had also been confirmed by the autopsy.

If only, if only…

The buoyant sound of four young girls heading toward her and Karla called a halt to their conversation. All four girls were close in age and were in their stocking feet.

Axel's older granddaughter, Holly, had auburn hair with a blend of lighter brown, natural highlights. Ivy, who was the younger one, had strawberry-blond hair. Paisley scrunchies gathered their long ponytails. Both wore jeans and green sweatshirts with Frosty the Snowman on the front.

Lynnie, Karla's daughter, had long blond hair that was captured in two braids. The nine-year-old had an angelic face but a spunky, spark-of-excitement personality.

"Girls, we appreciate that you don't want to track snow and mud into the library, but where did you leave your boots? I don't feel like going on a boot hunt when I pick you up," Elise let them know.

"Mrs. Charrette, you're funny," Lynnie giggled. "We placed them in the boot bins just inside the front door."

"Aunt Karla, our *bedstemor*, said we're going home with you," Holly announced before they took their seats.

"*Bedstemor*?" Elise questioned.

Karla turned her back to the girls and kept her voice low. "That's 'grandmother' in Danish. Axel is their grandfather, and Freja is their grandmother, even though they're in their forties and got married ten months ago. Get my sister to tell you the story," Karla suggested.

"I'd better get going. Don't want to keep Sebastian and Axel waiting."

Elise drove the five miles to the old bank barn, which had been totally renovated on the inside. The town had stipulated that the barn's exterior integrity had to be maintained, so only necessary repairs had been made. She recognized the two SUVs in the parking lot.

Before getting out, she used the mirror on the visor to refresh her lipstick. Her Aunt Britta had knit the red, white, and green variegated wool hat. Elise had never been a hat person, but she liked this one since the long cone tail draped around her neck like a scarf.

She got out of the warm car, and her breath blended with the cold air. The sky was a brilliant blue with only a few clouds. Her Uggs-covered feet crunched in the snow leading to the side entrance. She used her card key to get in and wiped her feet on the weather-guard runner just inside the door.

The owners had built an administrative area on the upper level, including a conference room, a music room, and a dance studio. Axel and Sebastian offered music lessons as an extension of the lessons taught in middle and high schools. Sebastian was the music teacher at the high school, so he was familiar with many of the kids.

The dance studio was overseen by a friend of Axel's. She was a former Rockette whose family owned a company that made musical instruments and sound equipment. Children could sign up for dance lessons for a nominal fee. The plan wasn't to make a profit but to spread the love of performing arts through music and dance.

Half of the upper level was occupied by the auditorium/theater, where live bands and musicals were performed. In addition to paid events, the event center held yearly dance recitals and school band festivals free of charge.

She walked down the corridor, drawn to the guitar music being played softly in the conference room. Two windows let light into the room. A dry-erase board listed the events for the next two months, and a smartboard occupied the opposite wall. They'd been practical in their scheduling, considering Old Man Winter didn't take their plans into consideration and liked to dump lots of snow every winter.

The first weekend in December would be a special performance of chamber music. *The Bells of St. Dickens*, a special play performed by the children, would be on Christmas Eve.

Sebastian was strumming a guitar. Although forty looked good on him, he could pass for years younger with his tall, slender build and coal-black hair. He'd taken to wearing the shadow of a dark beard that accented his square jaw. He'd unzipped his quilted vest, which he wore over a black and red flannel shirt.

Axel sat at the head of the conference table, flipping through photos on his iPad. She'd learned he was eight years older than Sebastian. His full head of black hair was combed straight back, except for a few strands that rested on his forehead. He wore a dark green and cream checked shirt with black jeans. Next to him was an oversized thermos of coffee and an assortment of kringle on a paper plate.

"Good morning."

"Hey," Sebastian greeted, setting the guitar in its case on the floor. "Thanks for meeting us here."

She set her puffy quilted coat and hat on the chair next to her before sitting down. Then, reaching into her bag, she removed her tablet.

Axel poured hot coffee into a cup and set it in front of her. "Kringle on behalf of my wife."

"Thank you. If you tell your wife this, I'll take the Fifth, but I'd never had kringle until I moved here."

"I won't tell her. Ever since she won that national kringle competition, her business has tripled. The pastries Lars and Jens, her assistant bakers, make are just as mouthwatering."

"The fudge sales have also doubled," Sebastian added. "Your aunt and uncle have taken over a good portion of making the fudge. My wife told me they hired three new salespeople to handle the holiday rush."

Elise helped herself to a slice of apple strudel kringle, and her taste buds exploded with flavor. Apple pie crepes were her favorite, but kringle pastry came in second. She wiped her mouth with a paper napkin. "Who wants to go first?"

"I'll start off." Axel picked up a slender controller for the smart screen, and a picture of his mini-train ride appeared. The black, steam-powered locomotive displayed a red, white, and blue fan flag. Smaller flags were attached to the roofline of the five other cars, which could each hold twenty passengers, and the red caboose.

"The train ride will be closed in January, February and March," Axel noted. "We'll work on adding seats in the caboose. The seasonal opening will be in April, with a special ride with the Easter Bunny. Elise's suggestion that we have themed July Fourth and Halloween excursions was a huge success that we'll be repeating."

"The train museum will open for its Christmas display the first week of December," Elise reminded them. "Roger, the head of the train club, and the other members will host the tours. Times and dates are listed on the website. After the first of the year, I'll post about the concerts and dates for the dance recitals. Seth Wolfington, the world-famous magician, has agreed to do a one-night-only magic show on Halloween weekend. He also said to say hello to you."

"I'll reach out and thank him personally," Axel said. He used some of our special lighting effects for his magic acts. These special train rides have drawn attention to our facility, and we've proven that the center pulls more visitors to Dickens. I'm a shop owner whose bottom line shows it's working. Once tourists visit the train museum, they visit my shop, Planes, Trains, and Automobiles. And 2 Sisters Kringle and Fudge are enjoying the same success."

Sebastian turned to Elise. "You know about the trouble the town gave us when we wanted to restore this barn."

Elise was well aware of the event's successes. The "but" factor in the owner's voice was alarming. "What aren't you telling me?"

"My wife attended the recent Chamber of Commerce meeting," Axel started. "They discussed promoting holiday events and special sales in town. At the end of the evening, two members confronted Freja about the special event we're planning. Their argument was that the flashy extravagance would draw shoppers away from Main Street."

"Apparently, someone learned about the details," Elise concluded.

Axel chuckled lightly. "They forgot my wife has red hair, and their petty comments ignited a small fire. Rather than escalate the situation, she said they were misinformed and that our events are still in the planning stages."

"People can be so selfish. It's not always about the bottom line! We're not making a cent," Sebastian said. "Through Axel's generosity, he covered the cost of the gazebo and all the display lights along the train route."

"Small-minded people!" Elise curled her fingers in frustration. "The children bring a toy to be shared with those who are less fortunate. Any monetary contribution will be added to the scholarship fund we established to help pay for music lessons, instrument rental, and dance lessons for kids who can't afford the fees."

A picture formed in Elise's head. "The evergreens will be magical with all the white lights. The snow will capture the rainbow of lights from the different figurines. We have a gorgeous Nativity and a menorah."

Elise's thoughts had taken off like an out-of-control freight train, and she swept a hand in the direction of Dickens Depot. "We need to remind people of Dickens's history, of the poet our town was named after."

"I've got something better," Axel said with a chuckle. "You two seem to forget that we have top-of-the-line video and holographic capabilities. Why not bring the famous poet back to life and project Charles Dickens into the center of the gazebo?"

"Axel, my friend, I know you're brilliant, but I think that's going a bit too far," Sebastian said.

"You two have lost it," Elise said, holding out a hand. "As of right now, our Holiday of Lights is on hold. On a different note, we should have a logo representing the arts and trains."

"I don't have a problem with that," Sebastian said. "Do you have someone in mind who can create something?"

"My son, Emile. He's an amazing graphic artist, but he's reluctant to share his work with anyone. This move has been difficult, so I wanted to give him a project that will focus on his craft and talent."

"It's funny you should say that," Sebastian said. "I have cafeteria duty three times a week. I saw Emile and Hailey sitting at a separate table. They were drawing on an artist's tablet. I was curious. They quickly closed the pad when they realized I could see what they were doing."

"As I mentioned, he's very shy about sharing his work, but he was enthused about creating a logo for the center. He'll create a few designs, and I'll show them to you."

"Perfect. If we're finished, I have to pick up my granddaughters at the library," Axel said.

She looked at both men. “According to the Full of Mischief Four, there’s a new flavor of fudge at 2 Sisters Kringle and Fudge. That’s where I’ll be heading after I pick up my children from the library.”

Their buzzing cell phones announced someone had approached the side door. Axel was the first one to check his phone. “I recognize who this is. Be right back.”

Two minutes later, he returned and wasn’t alone. “This is my old friend Giles DeLuc.”

The man held out a hand to Sebastian and shook. “We met when I visited Dickens last year.” And then he held out a hand to Elise. “Giles. And you are?”

“Elise Charrette.”

Chapter 2

I finally found you.

For once, luck was on his side. The photo he'd seen of Elise Charrette didn't do her justice. A twisted silver hairband kept her long, charcoal-black hair away from her lovely face, revealing silver hoop earrings. Her eyes were a soft blue-green, and her naturally long lashes accented her high cheekbones. Pink lip gloss made her lips appear dewy and fresh.

"Nice to meet you, Giles. I'm your neighbor. I saw you get out of your car, but I was leaving at the same time, so I didn't stop to introduce myself."

"You own that stone house?" *Of course, I already know that. You have a beautiful smile.* "Simone, the tabby, must belong to you since the next house is quite a distance down the road. At first, I thought she was a stray, but then I saw the collar with her name. I purchased a bag of cat treats for her."

"That was very nice of you," Elise said, "but don't fall for her feline schmoozing."

Axel said to Giles, "You let me know you were moving to Dickens, but you didn't say when."

"My life has been a whirlwind for the past ten months, but I officially moved into the house a few days ago. I stopped by the 2 Sisters to get kringle. Freja was helping customers and told me where to find you." He looked at everyone. "Sorry, I interrupted your meeting."

"No problem," Axel assured him. "You just caught me. I have to pick up Holly and Ivy from the library annex and take them to Freja. I'll be busy the rest of the day. We're setting up the holiday train display in the front window of Planes, Trains and Automobiles."

"I have to pick up Lynnie, also," Sebastian added.

"This is crazy. We're all going in the same direction. Why don't I pick up the Full of Mischief Four and take them to the shop?" Elise offered.

"Full of Mischief Four?" Giles asked.

Elise patted him on his arm. "My daughter, Sophie, Axel's granddaughters Holly, Ivy, and Lynnie, Sebastian's daughter, aka the Full of Mischief Four. They're harmless but feed on each other to get into trouble."

"If you can take Lynnie, that would be great," Sebastian said. "Jamie and his band are working on a new song for the holiday concert at the high school and asked me to assist with the arrangement."

Elise put on her coat and smiled at Giles. "If you've nothing to do tomorrow afternoon, we have a few unsold seats for our chamber music and poetry reading. See you around, neighbor."

Giles watched his neighbor rush off, leaving a trail of fresh air in her wake. “I feel like I’ve stepped into an alternate universe. Mischievous kids, fudge, band practice, window decorating, chamber music, and poetry.”

Sebastian laughed and picked up his coat. “Welcome to our world. Axel, I’ll see you tomorrow for supper,” he called out before leaving them alone.

“Giles, have a seat. I’ve got all of a half hour, and then I have to get to the shop.”

He lowered the zipper on his quilted jacket and sat next to his friend. “Is that woman always so full of energy?”

“Yes. Elise is very efficient and runs the place for us. She’s also a widow raising two wonderful kids.”

“When I pulled up, I was impressed at how much your event center has changed. The size of your parking area is quite large.”

“We opened the entertainment area in May with a popular country and western artist and were sold out. We vary the entertainment that’s drawing many visitors to Dickens. In July, we had an ‘all-aboard party’ to celebrate the opening of our mini train ride. Dickens Depot is in a separate section to the right of the event center. Future plans include a gift shop and a museum.

“Our Dickens Collectors Train Club is in the lower portion of this building. They oversee and maintain the displays. We offer group tours at a reduced rate, and the fees go directly into maintaining the displays."

"I'm impressed. What happens when it snows? Do you still run the train?"

"So far, we've had a mild winter with only a few inches of snow at a time. We have a small engine that clears the snow from the tracks. The cars are enclosed but not heated. The ride is only twenty minutes, but we supply lap robes. Hot chocolate and special treats are available at Dickens Depot, where we hold children's birthday parties. The Dickens Express will be closed for January, February, and March and reopen for our ride with the Easter Bunny in April."

"You do all this and run your hobby shop? Freja makes kringle and runs that business with her sister. You're workaholics."

"It may appear that way, but our children are given first priority in our lives. It's crazy, Giles, but I've never been happier."

There was something that needed to be said. *Get it out now and move on.* He locked his fingers, forming a tight grip, and couldn't look his friend in the face. "I've been carrying around a bucket of guilt. I never got back to you about doing that blood test to see if Holly and Ivy are my granddaughters."

"It no longer matters. Jens is happy to be a grandfather, and Lars is over the moon that he's an uncle. But since you brought up the subject, let's be honest. Why didn't you get back to me?"

He raised his head to look Axel in the face. "My business consumed my life. All I wanted to do was succeed and hear those whispers that my restaurants were the best. Call it ego, vanity, selfishness, thinking only of myself. I owe you an apology."

"You think your apology will make it all go away? Did you come back here expecting to reconnect with your friends like nothing happened?"

There was nothing like a friend who was honest and truthful. He couldn't sit any longer and began to pace. "This isn't an excuse, but have you ever made a mistake that had serious repercussions for someone else?"

Apparently, Giles had hit a soft spot with his question. His friend avoided direct eye contact. "Yes, one that affected the love of my life, but she's forgiven me."

"I'm very happy that you and Freja have found love. I've never been that lucky. In my drive to succeed, I hurt people but found out too late. It was a rude awakening, and I don't like myself right now. I'm going to apologize to Freja, Lars, and Jens. I'd also like to get to know your granddaughters." Now came the hardest part. "I didn't come here expecting forgiveness. Hoping, yes."

"That surprises me, but aren't you being a little hard on yourself?"

"No. I'm being honest. I lost touch with who I was and what I wanted to do with my life. I sold my portion of the restaurants and came to Dickens to start over."

"Of course." Axel nodded in comprehension. "You're the one opening the new café five stores down from my shop. Specializing in crepes is unique."

"That has been a dream of mine. I got the certificate of occupancy last week for Creperie de Dickens. I'll introduce a new cuisine to the locals and tourists. The recipes are from my ancestors."

"DeLuc. That isn't a French name."

"No, actually, it started as an Italian name. The story I was told is that when my relatives immigrated to America, their last name was DeLuca. They moved into a 'rough' neighborhood that looked down on Italians. They decided to drop the A to avoid being chastised. One of their daughters married a Frenchman."

"That's a colorful ancestry."

"Again, I apologize. When I said I wanted to start over, I meant it. When I owned the restaurants, people saw me for who I was and what I could do for them. I value your friendship, Freja's, Lars's, and Jens's. I'll work to prove myself and earn your friendship in return."

"Giles, I recognize we all make mistakes, and I admire you for being so open and honest. Friendships are precious. If you're sincere, show them through actions, and not words, what their friendship means to you."

Some of the guilt had lifted from his shoulders, but he had a long way to go.

"I'd like us to be good friends again." Axel put a hand on Giles's shoulder. "I'm about to toss you from the frying pan into the fire. Come to dinner tomorrow night at Sebastion and Karla's house at five p.m. They live across the street from Freja and me. We're celebrating Jens's birthday. Elise and her children will also be there. My cell phone number is the same. Be prepared for chaotic happiness."

This was more than he expected, so he held out a hand. "Thanks, Axel. I appreciate the invitation. What should I bring?"

"Here's some advice. You're probably thinking you should bring the kids presents, but don't. Friendship and respect are earned. Now, I've got to get going. I'll let Karla know to set an extra plate. I have to activate the building alarm, so we'll walk out together."

Giles waited until his friend drove away. For the first time in a year, he felt good. Carrying around the burden of confession had weighed him down. He rolled his shoulders. Better, but there was so much more to do. Hopefully, in the end, he'd like himself.

Before moving to Dickens, he'd purchased a used SUV. He did not want anything flashy to make his presence stand out, but he also wanted to have a four-wheel drive for when it snowed, like today. Having lived in Chicago, he was well-versed in dealing with snowy weather.

With the afternoon free, he took a slow drive into town, needing to learn more about the New England town that epitomized the holiday season.

Thanksgiving was only last week, but the stores were already decorated. Fresh pine garlands and red bows framed the entrances to the different shops. Flower boxes near the curb sprouted pine branches, large white pinecones, and red and green ornaments.

Last evening, he'd seen solar-powered white lights scattered throughout the branches. He enjoyed the Christmas music coming from the public speakers mounted atop the Victorian-style streetlights decorated with fresh wreaths.

Quiet, serene, unhurried.

As a new shop owner, he'd been added to the Chamber of Commerce email list and knew that the holiday season was a big deal to Dickens tourists, who arrived by the busload. The Chamber of Commerce always let the stores know when bus tours were scheduled, and he'd learned that Saturday sales were usually brisk. Three busloads of holiday shoppers were coming into town this morning.

He thought about what Axel had said about giving of himself and not showing up with gifts for the children. He agreed, but he should still bring the birthday boy a gift.

He drove around the block and parked in one of the spaces provided for shop owners. He walked down an alley between two stores. The snow crunched under his booted feet until he reached the snow-cleared sidewalk. Despite a few inches of snow, Dickens lived on. The road department did an excellent job keeping the streets cleared.

He paused to admire the front window of the Trim-A-Tree Shop. *Why not?*

The tinkle of a bell announced his arrival. Shoppers, holding small shopping baskets, were lined up at the register to pay for their purchases.

If Scrooge had been a real person and visited the shop early in his life, he wouldn't have become a hater of Christmas. The colorful lights, seasonal decorations, and pleasant smell of pine with a little spice filled the space. Music from *The Nutcracker* played softly overhead.

He walked slowly among the customers, who oohed and aahed at the decorations that could fill any room in the house. Two women blocked the aisle, and he couldn't help but hear what they were saying.

"Your granddaughter is going to love the ballerina ornament."

"Oh, thank you, Matilda. I can always count on you to have the perfect ornament."

If he hadn't known better, he'd swear Mrs. Claus had jumped off the pages of the poem *'Twas the Night Before Christmas*. A red mobcap trimmed in white lace covered her white curly hair. Her granny glasses didn't appear to be fake either.

"Welcome to Trim-A-Tree Shop," she said to him when the woman headed for the checkout counter. "I'm Matilda Cudworth, the shop owner.

Can I help you find an ornament or gift for someone special?"

"It's nice to meet you, Ms. Cudworth. I'm Giles DeLuc. I'll be opening Creperie de Dickens in two weeks."

"Welcome to Dickens, Giles, and please call me Matilda. I absolutely love crepes. I visited Paris twenty years ago. I never realized you could eat them for breakfast, lunch, dinner, or just as a delicious dessert."

"They're unique and a much-unappreciated dish. My menu is varied, and I know you will enjoy them. I love all your decorations and need to purchase a tree for my shop."

"You'll want traditional ornaments that reflect your shop's theme. I have exactly what you need. Follow me."

He hadn't given much thought to how he'd decorate his shop for the holidays—el Scrooge—but he would take the advice of an expert, Mrs. Claus.

She paused in front of a tree displaying ornaments representing nations all over the world. "What region of France are your relatives from?"

Until he'd decided to open a French creperie, his family's heritage had never been an issue. He'd have to seriously consider making an Italian crepe. "I've never researched the origin of my French background. These are all wonderful, but right now, I need a birthday gift for Jens Jorgenson."

She smiled, recognizing the name. "I'm very fond of Lars and Jens's pastries. The baking ornament tree is over here."

The ornament with a chef's hat and a rolling pin was perfect. He also selected a silver coin imprinted with a chef's hat and serving spoons.

"We can personalize the chef's hat ornament."

"I'd like that. Any chance you have gift bags, too?"

"We're a one-stop holiday shopping store."

A half-hour later, he walked out of the shop, happy with his purchases. He glanced up and observed the snow-laden clouds that had moved in. At one time, he'd been a closet meteorologist and astronomist, fascinated by the weather and stars. Nothing said he couldn't enjoy his old hobbies. The back of his house was wide open, offering great views for a telescope.

The tourist crowd was dwindling, and he walked half a block until he came to the store window covered by brown paper. The sign on the front door read "Coming Soon: Creperie de Dickens." A custom-carved wood sign will be mounted on the front of the storefront next week.

He used his key to unlock the door and locked it when he stepped inside. His chest swelled with pride. This small, intimate store was all his. He'd debated on going elegant with candles and flowers on the dozen square wood tables but had decided to leave things simple. The focus instead would be on the unique crepes he'd prepare.

The iron droplights with candlelight bulbs reflected on the marble-like floor. The walls were painted apple green. Behind the greeting station, a long planter filled with an assortment of fern plants separated the dining area from the kitchen's entrance.

He'd already hired two servers—sisters—and an assistant pastry chef. They were scheduled to meet with him on the Monday before opening. He'd already confirmed the food delivery. He was loving every minute of getting this shop off the ground.

He turned off the lights and walked out the back door, which was closer to where he'd parked. He'd barely started his SUV when the first snowflakes started to fall. He'd forgotten to stop at the grocery store to get something to fix for dinner. His laughter filled the interior of his car. He had eggs, flour, sugar, milk, and butter at the house.

An idea popped into his head. It was time to start making new friends and being hospitable. Homemade crepes would be an unexpected treat for his neighbors.

Elise stirred the beef stew so it wouldn't stick to the bottom of the pot. The biscuits she'd just taken out of the oven filled the kitchen with a mouthwatering scent.

She removed her apron, hung it on a hook behind the pantry door, and walked down the hall toward the parlor. The long table she kept under the front window for her plants was now against a wall. The space was wide open for their Christmas tree. Her friends had told her Gridley's Farm had the best selection of live trees. They'd always had an artificial tree when they lived in Chicago. Now, they couldn't wait to have a fresh tree. She wanted and needed this to be the best Christmas for her children.

Rather than walk up the stairs, she hollered, "Dinner is ready."

Two doors slamming told her the kids had heard her.

The knock on the front door was totally unexpected. Packages weren't delivered at six o'clock on a Saturday night. If they'd lived in the city, she would have been hesitant to open the door, worried that the money lenders had found them. The porch light was on so she could see their unexpected visitor.

She opened the door a little until she recognized her neighbor and then opened it fully. He'd rolled up the collar on his puffy jacket, and snowflakes had settled on the top of his knit cap. He was carrying a platter covered with foil.

"Hi, Elise. I hope I'm not interrupting."

"Come in," she invited and quickly closed the door behind him.

"I thought you might like to taste the crepes I made. They were warm a few minutes ago, but they'll still taste delicious heated up."

"You made crepes?"

Before he could answer, Sophie and Emile came running down the stairs and she introduced them to their neighbor. "This is Mr. Giles DeLuc, who moved in next door.

She turned back to their unexpected visitor. "This is Sophie and Emile, my children."

"Pleased to meet you both."

Simone made her presence known and brushed up against Giles's leg. "Hello to you, too."

"You didn't tell us we were getting company for supper," Emile challenged, focusing his attention on their neighbor.

She was somewhat taken aback by her son's manly, protective tone.

"I didn't mean to interrupt your dinner," Giles immediately apologized.

"Since you brought dessert, would you like to join us? We're having beef stew and homemade biscuits."

"I'd enjoy that very much. It's been a long time since I enjoyed a homemade meal. Do you want me to remove my boots?"

"No, you already wiped them on the rug. Give me your coat. The kitchen is straight ahead. Sophie, put the biscuits on the table, and, Emile, pour glasses of milk. Then take your seats at the table."

Their neighbor had set the foil-covered plate on the counter, but she still couldn't get over the fact that he'd made crepes.

"Have a seat," Elise said. "What would you like to drink? I have coffee, tea, milk, or water."

"Water would be fine." He looked around the kitchen. "Thanksgiving was only last week, but you've already started to put up Christmas decorations."

This afternoon, she'd draped a holly vine along the curtains and set out a reindeer-shaped napkin holder in the center of the table. The ceramic salt and pepper shakers were shaped like snowmen. "We found quite a number of plastic bins containing decorations in a crawlspace above Emile's room."

"It's really cool. There's a trapdoor in the ceiling in my bedroom."

"Mommy got a stepladder and stuck her head in the ceiling." Sophie crinkled her nose. "I thought it was spooky."

"Stone houses rarely have attics. I crawled up there and found quite a number of boxes, a few pieces of small furniture and what I believe are paintings wrapped in brown paper. The owner had posted a note saying the items were in the house when they moved in twenty years ago, so he thought they should stay with the house."

Elise ladled the stew into a soup tureen and carried it over to the table. "Help yourself to stew and biscuits."

The kids would normally chatter up a storm, but they were unusually quiet. Had she done the right thing by inviting their neighbor to join them for dinner?

Elise sliced open a biscuit and applied a little butter. “Giles, how do you like living in Dickens?”

“I feel like I stepped into Monet’s painting *Snow at Argenteuil*. The snow that settled on the ground this past hour transformed everything into a pristine, crystal world.”

Emile coughed and almost choked on the food he’d just put in his mouth. “You know about Monet?”

“I can’t paint to save my soul, but I’ve always been fascinated by the masters.”

“Have you ever been to the Louvre in Paris?” Emile asked.

“A number of times. I spend hours and hours each visit.”

“You’re lucky. I hope I get there someday.”

Elise was aware of her son’s disappointment. If she’d had the means, she’d take him to Paris to view, in person, the works of art that he loved.

“Do you paint?” Giles asked Emile.

“You mean like Monet, Rembrandt, or Picasso? No, but I like to study their work.”

“Emile, I think you’re selling yourself short.” You’re a wonderful artist. I’d challenge Monet, Rembrandt, or Picasso to draw the one-of-a-kind graphics you create.”

“Ah, Mom. You have to say that because you’re my mother.”

"I'm saying it because I'm proud of you. After supper, show your sketch pad to Mr. DeLuc."

"Unless you have something else to do this evening," she quickly said to their guest.

"I'd love to see Emile's work. Sophie, do you like painting, too?"

"Nah, I like soccer and having fun with my friends. We're going to be in the play *The Bells of St. Dickens*. Do you have kids, Mr. DeLuc?"

"No. Sadly, I've never been a father."

Elise appreciated that he engaged her children in conversation while enjoying his dinner.

"That was delicious," he said, wiping his mouth with a red paper napkin.

"Kids, Mr. DeLuc brought dessert. We'll have it in a little while. Scrape your plates and put them in the sink. You're off KP this evening."

"What did you bring, Mr. DeLuc?" Sophie asked, setting her utensils in her empty bowl.

"Please, call me Giles."

Emile shook his head. "That's not polite. Mom said we have to be respectful to old people."

Elise winced inwardly at the "old people" comment. She judged Giles to be in his early forties, a couple of years older than her. His hair was medium chocolate brown, longer on top, and casually brushed back from his forehead. The sides were trimmed close, and she noticed a few gray hairs above his ears. Like her boss, the shadow of a dark beard accented his rounded jaw. Flecks of gold speckled his hazel eyes. He also had a great smile.

"You can call him Mr. Giles," she told her children.

"So, what did you bring, Mr. Giles?" Sophie asked.

His lips formed a big smile. "It's a special treat. Crepes."

"I bet they're not as good as my mom's," Sophie challenged.

Chapter 3

"Giles, I'm sorry for her rude comment, but crepes are a standard food item around here."

He tilted his head to the side. "Why should I be surprised? Your last name is French. Have you ever traced your heritage?"

"My family emigrated from Paris in the late 1800s, and my late husband's family originated from Marseille."

"I've visited there several times. I always make it a point to get madeleines, the city's signature treat. They're a shell-shaped sweet sponge cake cookie. The almond-flavored ones are the best."

"I've had them, not in France, but they go perfectly with a cup of tea. It sounds like you've traveled a lot."

"The company that I used to work for was international, so I got to see a lot of the world. Who taught you to make crepes?"

"My grandmother had a small creperie, only open four days a week. I'd go there directly from school and help her and my mother. People loved her crepes so much that they would order some to take home. When she passed, my parents took over and expanded the creperie to five days a week. Of course, I was expected to help."

She hesitated, blinking a film of tears from her eyes. "That's where I met my husband. The shop was so busy they had to hire help. He was a pâtissier by trade, but his real love was making crepes. His dream was to open a creperie and offer unique dishes for lunch and dinner. Unfortunately, he was killed in a car accident."

"I'm so sorry, Elise. How long have you been living in Dickens?"

"We moved here in March. I was working for an event planner and my Aunt Britta let me know about an opening at the new event center. She and my Uncle Dane work at 2 Sisters Kringle and Fudge."

"I was there yesterday and couldn't resist purchasing some of their signature chocolate fudge. It must be nice having relatives close by."

"That's another reason why we moved here. I love my job since I can work from home, care for my children, and see some fantastic shows. Now, enough about me. Tell me more about Giles DeLuc."

"I visited Axel and Freja and fell in love with Dickens. Actually, I met Freja, Lars, and Jens when they were going to school in New York. I was under a lot of pressure from my other job, so I decided to follow my dream. I'm opening Creperie de Dickens in two weeks. It's five shops away from Planes, Trains and Automobiles."

"Oh, Giles, that's wonderful. I've been so busy I haven't taken the time to go downtown. You'll be enhancing the flavor experiences for the residents and visitors of Dickens."

"I'm not the only one who is hyping the culture in Dickens. Axel told me about the wonderful variety of shows you've scheduled for the center."

Warmth made her cheeks a little red. "I try to have a variety of shows to accommodate everyone's taste in entertainment. I hope you join us tomorrow for the chamber music and poetry reading. The performance will be followed by tea and crumpets."

He raised a brow. "Tea and crumpets. For real?"

"Yes."

"I didn't realize Dickens was so sophisticated."

"There's a little more to it, but you have to promise not to tell anyone."

He held up a hand, palm out. "You have my word."

"Axel and Sebastian were given a hard time when they initiated their plans for an event center. The naysayers said it would bring the wrong element to their quaint town. One of the wives of the council members inquired about having chamber music. They assured her that was a possibility."

"You apparently made it happen."

"My eyes were opened to a whole new avenue of entertainment when I started researching chamber music. There is a Chamber Music Society of

Lincoln Center in NYC. Playing chamber music requires musical skills that differ from those required for solo or symphonic works. The instruments will include a viola, three violins, a clarinet, a bass, and a piano. This is the group's second performance here this year. The musicians are wonderful. Along with scores written by Bach, Mozart, and Gershwin, their holiday show will include Christmas and Hanukkah songs. Classic prose about the holidays will be read."

"Have you sold many tickets?"

"We're ninety percent sold, but I expect walk-ins to fill the rest of the seats."

"I'm truly impressed. When I lived in New York, I never took the time to visit Lincoln Center. I'll take advantage of the citizens of Dickens, who instill culture and refined entertainment."

"I promise you'll love the performance. I just thought of something else. The mayor, members of the Chamber of Commerce, and local media will be attending. This will give you the opportunity to meet them and promote your shop. They're very nice, but without naming names, some of their noses point upward."

"Thanks for letting me know. What's the dress code since this sounds highbrow?"

"Some of the men wear suits and ties, while the ladies get very dressed up."

"I haven't worn a dress shirt and a tie in a long time."

Elise felt sorry for him. "A sweater is fine, but nix the jeans."

"That, I can handle."

"After the show, I'll give you a tour of the Dickens Depot."

"I'd like to see that. Who will be watching the children?"

"Emile works part-time at the event center and will be with me. I'm dropping Sophie off at Karla's house. We're invited to the birthday dinner they're having for Jens."

"I've also been invited. I stopped by the Trim-A-Tree Shop to get Jens a gift. I met Matilda and was overwhelmed by the variety of trees and ornaments. I plan to get an artificial tree for the shop. Her suggestion was to hang ornaments with a French flavor."

Elise was probably being a bit forward, considering they'd just met, but she asked anyway. "What about a tree for your house?"

"I haven't thought that far."

"We will be getting a Christmas tree from Gridley's Farm next Saturday, which will be a new experience for us. I've been told the farm has a wonderful petting zoo, too."

"If you don't mind, I'd like to join you. I've never had a fresh tree. I can also help you bring your tree into the house."

"We'd appreciate your help."

"Visiting a petting zoo will be another first." Giles expelled a heavy sigh. "This may sound crazy, but everyday life has been going on around me, but I've never stopped, looked, heard, or listened.

Moving to Dickens has changed so much for me. I walk outside at night and see millions of stars. The moon is a bright ball in the sky. I heard church bells ringing on Sunday morning. When I purchased a bag of treats for Simone, someone was buying a bag of wild bird feed. It never dawned on me that the birds need food in the winter, too."

He blushed slightly. "Sorry for rambling. Thanks for listening."

"Anytime. We've been talking so much I never started the coffee."

"My evening is free. How about I help you wash the dishes, and then we can enjoy dessert? I'd also like to see Emile's drawings."

"I appreciate that you want to help, but you're a guest."

He gave her a little smile. "I was when I walked in the door, but now I'd like to be considered a good friend."

"Friend it is."

She approached the sink, and he followed. "The house is old, and I don't have a dishwasher."

"I think your home is warm, cozy, and welcoming."

"That's what I think, too. I didn't have much money to put down on a house. Stone houses don't come cheap, but this one needs a lot of work. The owner wanted to sell it quickly, and we needed a place to live." She turned on the hot water, and a couple of seconds later, the pipes started to knock.

He raised his head and slowly scanned the ceiling. “Tell me you don’t have ghosts in the walls.”

“No, just pipes that sing and knock,” she explained with a little chuckle. “We’ve gotten used to the house with a unique name—Ringing Rocks House. When you tap on certain rocks, they ring, but we’ve never tried it.”

Giles leaned against the counter and folded his arms over his chest. “I’ve never heard of such a thing. Did the previous owner provide any history about the house?”

“If you mean historical background, no. I’ve been so busy creating a life for my children that I never gave any thought to researching information about ringing rocks.”

Giles removed the dishtowel from the rack attached to the cabinet by the sink and started drying the dishes. “My house is boring compared to yours. It’s my first house. I’ve always lived in a high-rise. Everything was done for me, from decorating to taking out the garbage. Building from scratch would have taken too long, so I purchased a modular. I’m just starting to get pieces of furniture. My main focus has been setting up my creperie.”

When he finished drying, she put the dishes in the cabinet. “Thanks for helping clean up. Let me get the kids.”

“While you do that, I’ll warm the crepes in the microwave and pour the coffee.”

She watched him place each warmed crepe on a serving plate, treating each one like he was a master craftsman who'd sculpted it to perfection. This told her he took pride in what he'd prepared.

When Elise took her first bite of crepe, she wasn't prepared for her tongue to fall in love. It was light, flavorful, and pure nirvana. He'd added a little honey, and she detected the flavor of a chocolate bean, but she hadn't encountered any crunchy granules.

She set her fork down after eating the entire crepe. "Giles, these are so delicious. I catch the intense flavor of real cacao."

The smile he gave her said he was quite pleased with her comment. "You have sharp, distinctive taste buds. Those will be one of my special dessert crepes. I use real cacao beans. Many people regard the best cocoa beans in the world are grown in South America. The Caribbean island of Trinidad grows only Trinitario cacao, a highly flavorful type of cacao developed on the island hundreds of years ago."

"Mr. Giles, these are good," Sophie said, "but I'd like to have French vanilla ice cream with mine."

"Thank you, Sophie. I'll follow your suggestion and serve them with French vanilla ice cream. As a thank-you for the idea, your first dessert crepe will be on me when you come into my shop."

"Giles, you don't have to do that," Elise said.

"Elise, it's my pleasure, and this is very important. Seeing my crepes from the standpoint of a child's taste means a great deal. I haven't heard your opinion, Emile. What do you think?"

"These are really good, but if you use the cacao beans, I'd like it with chocolate ice cream."

"I love both your ideas," he said with a big smile. "If you're done with dessert, I'd love to see your drawings."

"Let me get my sketch pad," Emile said and hurried upstairs.

"Mom, I've seen his stuff. Can I go upstairs and work on my project?"

This was the first she'd heard of any project her daughter was working on. "What project?"

"We're making special decorations to hang up for Mr. Jens's birthday party."

"All right. Try not to make a mess." *Sure, and it won't snow in January in New England.*

"Thanks for the crepes, Mr. Giles. See you around."

"Your children are delightful and have wonderful manners."

"Thank you. They've suffered emotionally from their father's death, and it's been hard raising them alone. Can I give you a refill on your coffee?"

"Please. From what I've seen, you're a wonderful single mom, and they appear to be happy."

Emile reappeared and set a large portfolio on the table, quickly explaining, "Some are rough sketches, and others I've filled in with bold colors."

Elise stirred her coffee, which didn't need stirring. *Please let Giles be kind.*

Their neighbor slowly turned the pages, studying each drawing without saying a word. She could feel the subdued excitement coming from her son, who was looking for approval.

When he'd started drawing, Emile had asked if she thought people would like his work. She'd been honest right from the beginning. She thought his work was outstanding, but she'd told him that if someone criticized his work, he shouldn't take it as a hurtful comment. Come right back, she'd said, and ask what they didn't like about it. He should take it as a learning experience if they give him constructive criticism. He should try to see his work through their eyes, acknowledge what they see, and see how he could improve on the drawing.

"Emile, the characters are so alive they practically jump off the pages. The spectrum of colors is extraordinary—chartreuse, gold, ink blue, chocolate brown, and blood red. Where do you get the ideas for your unique characters?"

"My friends," he replied with a chuckle.

Giles jerked back his head, looking at Emile. "Your friends look like this?"

"No, it's their personalities that inspire the characters. Buddy is always eating chocolate, so chocolate syrup oozes from his skin, and his fangs are dark brown. *Demons of Candyland* is about these weird monsters who are deformed pieces of candy made by the manufacturer."

"I'm truly overwhelmed. Candy-influenced monsters. What happened to just getting rotten teeth from eating too many sweets?"

The despondent look on Emile's face said he regretted sharing his work with an adult who would never understand. *Emile, take pride in your work and ask what he doesn't like about it.* Elise silently implored.

Emile closed the portfolio. "I knew you wouldn't understand, but my mom told me if someone doesn't like my work, I should ask them why and take criticism as a learning curve."

"What?" Giles jerked back in the chair, wide-eyed. "Are you kidding me? I'm an adult who is way past understanding teen pop culture, but I think your drawings are outstanding!"

"You mean it?"

"Emile, I've studied art, but I'll admit I haven't studied graphic art. You're very talented. I have a friend who owns a gallery in Chicago and is also a professor of art. He knows everyone in the business and then some. Let me make a call. Maybe he can point us in the right direction and suggest courses you could take if you want to pursue your love of art on a professional level."

"Mr. Giles, that would be awesome!"

Elise put a hand on Emile's shoulder. "Be prepared for some negative feedback."

"Either way, Emile, keep drawing." Giles wiggled his eyebrows. "Is there any chance I can become a character?"

"Really?"

"I'd love it. My favorite candy is red licorice."

"I'll see what I can do," Emile said, holding out his hand. "Thanks for being honest with me. If you need someone to clear your driveway when it snows, I'll help you—no charge. We have a snowblower."

"I'd appreciate that, and you'll not do it for free."

"Thanks again. Mom, I've got to call Hailey and tell her that Mr. Giles likes my work. He's going to call a gallery owner in Chicago! Maybe this guy can look at Hailey's drawings, too!"

"I can't thank you enough," Elise said when she was alone with Giles. "I haven't seen him this happy in a long time. He doesn't talk about it, but I know he misses his dad."

"I can empathize with Emile's pain. My father was my best friend. He and my mother passed fifteen years ago."

"No other family?"

"My brother died eighteen months ago from COPD. He was a heavy smoker. He was married, but they never had any children. Spending time with you and your children has brought me great joy. I've never had a family of my own, so I've missed a great deal."

"Feel free to enjoy the craziness of this family anytime. Will I see you at the concert tomorrow?"

"Absolutely." He stood but drank the last of his coffee. "Dinner was delicious. I can't tell you when I've had a more enjoyable evening. I hope you'll enjoy the rest of the crepes."

"We will. The kids will have them for breakfast," Elise said as she walked him to the front door. "We never got to look at the paintings I found in the attic. We'll save that for the next time."

As she said this, she realized that she really did hope to spend another enjoyable evening with him.

"I'll take that as an invitation and gladly accept."

He zipped his heavy jacket and pulled the knit cap low enough to cover the tops of his ears. "There will definitely be a next time. Night, Ms. Elise."

She watched him walk down the short walkway connecting to her driveway. He turned and waved. Tonight had been a lot of fun, and Giles DeLuc was a delightful surprise.

She went upstairs to check on Sophie.

Her daughter was sitting at the desk she'd found in the basement and was currently gluing silver glitter to balloons. Elise cringed. Sophie had more glitter on her face and in her hair than on the balloons, but she'd had the forethought to cover the top of the desk with newspaper.

"Sophie! What a mess! Where did you get that glitter?"

"From Lynnie. We're all making special balloons for tomorrow night. Mine are silver, Lynnie's are red, Holly's are gold, and Ivy's are green."

"That's very thoughtful of you, but we need to clean this up. You have to take a shower. Then, we'll continue reading your book, The Carpenter's Gift, before bed."

They put the six balloons in a large garbage bag, ready to be transported to the birthday party. The hardest part was getting the glitter off the hardwood floor.

A half-hour later, Sophie hopped onto the bed. The soft fleece onesie she'd put on after her shower was decorated with Santa elves and reindeer.

"Get under the covers, and I'll brush and braid your hair."

Elise sat on the edge of the bed and slowly ran the brush through her daughter's slightly damp hair. She'd always loved the scent of baby powder, so she'd been glad to find a shampoo with a similar scent. Their mother-daughter time was the perfect way to end the day. She'd enjoyed these special moments when her mother had brushed her hair as a little girl.

"Did you have fun today?"

"I had a good time at the library with my friends. Mom, are you going on a date?"

Elise paused with the brush in midair. "Where did you get that idea?"

"Mr. Giles is very nice. His crepes are very good, too. I like him. He didn't ask for any wine."

Elise didn't like where this was going. "I didn't offer him any wine because I don't have any in the house."

"That's good because Daddy used to drink too much wine. Then he'd fall down or sleep on the couch. He never did anything with us. Sometimes, he was grumpy and grouchy."

Elise was taken aback by her daughter's comments about her father. Her children had never told her that their father's behavior upset them. Claude had worked a great deal. When he *had* been home, he'd never taken the time to enjoy or interact with his children. It broke her heart that Sophie's memory of her father was so negative.

"Has Emile ever said anything about your father?"

"No, but he told me that he found a bunch of bottles of wine in the basement closet at our old house. He dumped them out, refilled them with colored water, and put them back."

Admitting she was shocked would be an understatement. How had all this gone on in her home without her knowing?

"Your daddy was a wonderful man, but he had a problem. He might not have said it, but he loved you and Emile. When we go to church tomorrow, we should pray for him."

"That's a good idea. I'll tell him I miss him, too. So, are you going to go on a date with Mr. Giles?"

How quickly this child could switch from one subject to another. "Sophie, I don't have time to go on a date. My life is full with you and Emile. I love my job. We've got a wonderful family with Aunt Britta and Uncle Dane. We have lots of friends. What more could I ask for?"

"Okay, if you say so. Now I'm ready to read the story. Mom, we should plant a pinecone in the backyard. Like in the story, it will grow big, and the wood will go to a needy family to build a house."

"That's a beautiful idea. We'll look for a pinecone next week at Gridley's. It's my turn to read a chapter."

She loved the story about Henry and his father selling Christmas trees in New York City during the Depression. The young boy gave a tree to construction workers building Rockefeller Center. Through the kindness of the workers, the boy's family was given a warm home to replace their old, drafty shack. Years later, as an old man, Henry repaid the original gift by donating an enormous tree that had grown from the pinecone from the original Rockefeller tree. Each year, the tree on display was taken to a mill, and the wood was used to build a home for a family in need.

After saying good night to Emile, Elise took a shower and snuggled under the down-filled quilt covering her bed. The two windows were covered with lace shades, but she'd framed them in champagne-beige homespun drapes. Beige and rust-throw carpets decorated the dark mahogany wood floors. The cherrywood bedroom set had belonged to her parents. The flowery wallpaper had faded over the years, but she liked the "old" look.

Sophie's comment was troubling and brought back a lot of old hurts. *Daddy used to drink too much wine. Then he'd fall down or sleep on the couch. Sometimes, he was grumpy and grouchy.*

She'd tried hard to create a happy, secure family atmosphere for her children. Claude had been a wonderful pastry chef. Due to his skills, her parents' creperie was still a big success. They had a very comfortable income and didn't need a bigger place. He'd never taken the time to be a "father" to their children or understand what being a family was all about. He'd had big dreams that had cost a lot of money, initiating many arguments that had ruined their marriage.

But when it had all fallen apart, she had moved on and started a new, happy life with her children. Every night, she prayed that the people from whom he had borrowed so much money would not find them.

Her daughter's other comment—*are you going to go on a date?*—wasn't troubling at all. Giles DeLuc was very nice, and she enjoyed his company. He'd dried the dishes and loved her Ringing Rocks House. They shared French ancestry, and both made crepes. He'd asked about her job at the event center.

He'd recognized Emile's talent and was going to reach out to someone who could give him direction.

Would she go out on a date if he asked? Maybe, but she'd prefer to learn more about her boss's old friend.

Chapter 4

Elise stood back to double-check the setup for the Tea and Crumpets get-together that would follow the show. She'd gone for tasteful/elegant and decided she'd hit the mark. This was the first high-end get-together she'd organized for the center, so she needed to make sure everything was perfect. They were using the small meeting room just off the main entrance.

The two dessert tables were covered with the lace tablecloths she'd found in her house, and she'd placed red liners underneath for a holiday flair. The centerpieces were thin white birch branches and pokes of green holly with red berries. She'd wound tiny white lights around the stems cradled in tall crystal vases.

Karla had donated the silver candlesticks, which she and Sebastian had gotten for a wedding gift, and red candles. The patterns on the china teacups and teapots varied since she'd borrowed them from Karla, Freja, and Aunt Britta.

A variety of finger desserts were artfully displayed on faux-silver stacking tiers. The crumpets were on their own trays. Orange marmalade, strawberry preserves, slices of lemon, cream, and sugar cubes were also on the table.

As soon as the show was over, she poured hot water over the tea infusers in the six china teapots lined up on the table. Anticipating that not all of the twenty-five attendees would like tea, a punchbowl with a special holiday punch infused with candied cranberries sat at the end of the table.

A knock on the door had her turning around. Seeing Giles, a smile filled her face. He'd taken her advice and wore a black leather sports jacket over a white turtleneck sweater. His trousers were a dark charcoal. The handsome package caused her heart to do a number of flip-flops. He was carrying a foil-covered tray. Whatever he'd brought teased her taste buds.

"Hi, I'm so glad you were able to attend."

"After I paid for my ticket, I saw Emile handing out programs. He told me where to find you."

"What did you bring?" she said, approaching him.

"You mentioned last evening how important this event is to you and the center, so I thought I'd add to your elegance. I made a hundred mini crepes that can be served at room temperature. I make my own sauces, and these are flavored with faux Grand Marnier and drizzled with dark chocolate. They can be eaten by hand, but I brought clear plastic forks. Say no if you don't want them or if I'm being too forward."

He didn't say, *This is a way to promote my creperie.* He was doing it for her and his friends.

"That was very thoughtful of you. The delicacy will be perfect." She took the tray from his hands and set it on the table close to the other treats. "Can I take a peek?"

"Sure." He lifted the edge of the foil and selected one. "Be my official taster."

Like last evening, the flavor and lightness of the pancake exploded on her tongue. "Oh my, these are really good. I love the subtle taste of orange, and the dark chocolate brings everything together. You'll have a stampede to your creperie. Did you bring business cards?"

"Your approval is very much appreciated." He shook his head. "I didn't bring any promotional items. Trying to ride the center's coattails would be unethical, and this is *your* event. I don't plan to attend Tea and Crumpets since I didn't pay the additional fee."

"I appreciate your honesty and integrity. We'll consider your crepes the price of your admission to the tea. Join us after the chamber music show, and I'll introduce you to some of the prominent citizens of Dickens and mention your new restaurant. Your crepes will be well received."

"Thank you. You look lovely."

The formality of the event called for a long black skirt paired with a silky red long-sleeved blouse. She'd drawn her hair up on one side and secured it with a small piece of holy and a wide hairclip.

“Thank you. You look very nice, too.

“Thanks. I recognized Jamie Nielson when I got here.”

“Jamie assists the stage manager with the audio and lights. Emile hands out programs and does a walkthrough after the shows to collect garbage. Jamie’s girlfriend, Ashley, runs the concession stand, but we didn’t open it for this event. For the larger events, we bring in additional help.”

“I think it’s wonderful that you’re giving them the opportunity to earn some money.” He walked closer to the table. “Your food presentation looks beautiful and appetizing, right down to the crumpets.”

“When I asked Leslie, the owner of Leslie’s Bakes and More, if she could make crumpets for a special event, she laughed. Many people don’t know what crumpets are, but she assured me there wouldn’t be a problem. She once worked in a tearoom where they made all the desserts, including crumpets.”

“I’ve had the opportunity to enjoy tea in London, so I know what they are. Hers look perfect.”

“Care to enlighten me? I’ve never seen or tasted one before.”

“A crumpet is a small griddle bread made from an unsweetened batter of water or milk, flour, and yeast. The batter is loose, so a cooked crumpet has a spongy interior texture. They’re usually cooked inside a crumpet ring mold.”

"When I have tea, my preference is scones, orange marmalade, and clotted cream, but I'll definitely be tasting the crumpets." Elise checked her watch. "Better take your seat. We'll be starting in ten minutes."

"I hope you don't mind, but Emile asked if he could sit next to me. I double-checked with Jamie about the seating. Since I'm sitting so far back, the seat next to mine is empty."

"That's very nice of you. Just an FYI. The surround sound is amazing, no matter where you sit in the theater. See you after the show."

Elise walked into the lobby and headed for Emile. All of the attendants had been given white shirts, red vests and engraved name tags. The logo he planned to design would look great just under his name badge.

"Emile, I'm so proud of you." She snuck in a quick hug, already knowing she'd be embarrassing him.

"Mom, I only have five programs left."

"That's fine. The show will start in a few minutes, so we shouldn't sell any more tickets."

"I'm sitting next to Mr. Giles during the show if that's okay with you. He doesn't have any family or many friends here in Dickens, so I didn't want him to feel alone."

"He already told me, and that's very kind of you."

A rush of cold air swept into the lobby, and she turned to see Sebastian and Axel coming through the front door. Both looked very nice in black suits and ties with white shirts.

"You're cutting it close. Give me your coats, and I'll hang them up in the office."

"The parking lot is full," Axel pointed out, removing his fleece-lined jacket. "Who knew that many people would be interested in chamber music?"

"You and I know it's a long-forgotten art," Sebastion commented.

Emile handed them each a program. "Enjoy the show."

"We sure will." Axel winked.

As soon as the houselights dimmed, Elise sat in the last row on the side aisle. There were only four unsold seats. When planning the events, they tried to vary the shows to please everyone. Most of the events had been profitable, but for a couple, they barely broke even.

The conductor stood center stage, dressed in a tuxedo with a red bow tie. The audience gave him a courteous round of applause. He announced the composer of the first songs—selections from Tchaikovsky's *The Nutcracker*, including "Waltz of the Flowers," "March of the Toy Soldiers," and "Dance of the Sugar Plum Fairy"—and briefly explained their origins.

The theater's sound system made the room come alive. When the last note for "Dance of the Sugar Plum Fairy" faded, Elise realized tears were running down her cheeks.

The performance's second selection was "Ode to Joy." The conductor explained that it wasn't written as a Christmas song but was based on Friedrich Schiller's poem of the same name, which stressed hope, peace, and unity. At the very end, a violin played softly in the background while a number of verses from the poem were read.

Mozart's "Sleigh Ride" from *Three German Dances* gave the listener the feeling of traveling on the snow-covered hills in a sleigh.

The next presentation was a reading of "Love Came Down at Christmas," a poem by Christina Rossetti that was published in 1885.

Love came down at Christmas,
Love all lovely, Love Divine,
Love was born at Christmas,
Star and Angels gave the sign…

Once again, Elise shed more tears when the reading was finished.

She looked at the program with blurred vision, already knowing they were about to change things up with a little bit of country and Western music. First up was "Tennessee Christmas," a song originally sung by Amy Grant.

They played "Light One Candle," a Hanukkah song Peter, Paul, and Mary made popular, followed by "O Holy Night."

Elise was already anticipating the finale that would put the seal on this beautiful show. She hadn't shared her plans with anyone, not even Axel or Sebastian.

They were fortunate to have Shawn Murphy as the sound and lighting engineer. The fifty-five-year-old had worked Broadway productions in New York City. When the theaters had shut down because of the COVID-19 pandemic, he'd moved closer to his great-aunt, Matilda Cudworth. He also doubled as stage manager. Shawn had enlisted the help of Jamie Nielsen for Elise's surprise but had sworn him to secrecy.

Jamie pushed a red wingback armchair onto the stage. A few gasps filled the audience when Matilda Cudworth strolled onto the stage dressed as Mrs. Claus. She draped a thin blanket over her lap and started reading *'Twas the Night Before Christmas*. She'd just finished reading the poem when the musicians started playing Irving Berlin's "White Christmas."

"Wait for it," Elise said out loud.

Oohs and aahs filled the room when it started to "snow." The imitation snowflakes were tiny pieces of soapy foam that immediately melted when they touched a surface, whether it was skin or something else. The theatergoers were so enthused that they held up their hands to try to catch the snowflakes.

The ensemble got a standing ovation. The show had been overwhelming and infused everyone with the holiday spirit.

Elise sent a quick text to Shawn. *The lights, sounds, and snow are outstanding! They're just perfect. Thank you.*

My pleasure, considering the top-of-the-line equipment you let me play with.

Give me five minutes, then start the longhair background music.

The audience was clapping when she made a hasty exit and hurried to the conference room to prepare the tea.

Axel and Sebastian came in, all smiles.

“Did you like my surprise?” she asked.

“You outdid yourself on this one,” Sebastian said. “I noticed you took advantage of the ‘extra’ features we added to our production equipment. We thanked Shawn for doing a great job. I’ll be right back.”

As Sebastian slipped away, Axel continued to smile. “People are already asking when we’ll have another chamber music event.”

“I’m sure we’ll be able to have another one, but I have to check our schedule. Before the guests arrive, we need to be on the same page if we’re asked about the Dickens Holiday of Lights.”

“You mean the Charles Dickens page?” Axel teased. “We’ll continue to stress the historical element of the tracks, the trains, the depot that serviced the area. We might mention we have a surprise and leave it at that.”

“What surprise?” Sebastian asked, returning with a cup of punch and crepes in hand.

“Why, the holographic appearance of Charles Dickens. Where did the crepes come from?” Axel asked.

"Giles," Elise said. "He wanted to contribute something to add a little pizzazz to our reception."

"I didn't realize he was attending the show," Sebastian said.

"He sat at the back with Emile. He'll be joining us for tea."

Their conversation ended when the guests filtered into the room. The ladies and a few gentlemen went for the tea. Sebastian and Axel held court with two different groups. All were nodding, so it appeared they agreed with whatever the owners were saying.

While pouring the tea, she kept glancing at the entrance, wondering where Giles was.

She'd just refilled one of the teapots when the three gossip queens approached. Elise wondered if they consulted one another about what to wear before they attended an event. Viola Hughes, Sadie Prince, and Tillie Doyle were lifelong friends who played bridge every week and were members of the gardening and senior citizens clubs.

The three wore two-piece hunter-green dresses with large faux gold buttons, reminding Elise of the buttons on a double-breasted military jacket. They'd even paired up their gold jewelry. Their white hair was styled similarly in soft waves, giving each woman a refined look. They'd gone a little heavy on the makeup.

"Elise, this reception is fabulous," Sadie said. "The background music is lovely. You outdid yourself with the crumpets. Using delicate china teacups elevates the flavor of the tea with each sip."

'Elevates the flavor of the tea.' Jeez. "Thank you, Sadie. I appreciate your compliment." Sadie's husband, Benson, was head of the Department of Public Works. He'd made a personal appearance several times during the construction of the event center to ensure that the construction vehicles entering and exiting the site didn't damage the main road, which his department was responsible for maintaining. He'd been touting his position, but she'd seen right through his excuse. He'd really come by to find out what was going on.

"Leslie from Leslie's Bakes and More did such a wonderful job on the desserts, especially the crepes," Sadie said.

"These crepes are divine," Tillie Doyle agreed.

Elise noted that Tillie had three on her plate. The woman's husband, Thaddeus, was on the town council and head of the Ways and Means Committee. He was one of those who'd had the most objections about the profitability of the center and the supposed burden it would put on the taxpayers. She knew for a fact that Axel's pockets were quite deep, and he'd never gone to the town for funding. He also made sure the contractors had secured all of the required permits and that the on-site inspections had been completed. All of the certificates were in a binder she'd personally put together.

Viola Hughes, head of the Chamber of Commerce, raised her nose a little higher. “We’re about to get some sophistication on Main Street. I know all about Creperie de Dickens. My husband has met Giles DeLuc. Giles stopped in to get an application to be a member of the Chamber of Commerce, but I just missed him. Harry said he’s quite refined, a world traveler. He’s quite knowledgeable about art and has been to the Louvre.”

Elise had determined Viola was a snob, but she had to work with these people. She was about to make her excuses when Giles finally walked in. Her eyes widened in surprise. What had happened to Mr. Neat Sophistication? He’d discarded his leather jacket and turtleneck and now wore a T-shirt that sported the name of a rock band called Cosmic Jammers.

He gave them a friendly smile. “Ladies, my apologies.”

He looked at Elise. “Sorry, I’m late to the party. I helped Emile when he walked through the aisles to pick up trash, including a bunch of candy wrappers some inconsiderate people dropped on the floor.”

Elise looked to the ceiling and rolled her eyes. It took everything in her not to burst out laughing. The inconsiderate candyholics were standing right in front of them. The three ladies had a thing for three different kinds of Werther’s caramels. She might suggest to her son that he add a trio of candyholics to his fictional characters.

"Then Jamie got a flat tire," Giles continued. "He had a hard time getting the lug nuts off and didn't want to bother his father. I had a better wrench, so I helped him change his tire. I didn't want to get my white sweater dirty, so Jamie had this T-shirt in the back of his car and let me borrow it."

The three ladies kept staring at the "gentleman," who certainly wasn't dressed for this prestigious tea. Personally, she thought he looked adorable and quite handsome.

"Elise, would you mind introducing me to these lovely ladies?" Giles asked.

"Giles DeLuc, I'd like you to meet Viola Hughes, Sadie Prince, and Tillie Doyle, three of Dickens's most prominent citizens."

He acknowledged Viola while holding out his hand. "Ms. Hughes, I had the pleasure of meeting your husband the other day. Harry explained that you're head of the Chamber of Commerce. I look forward to working with you."

If Viola had been an ice cube, she would have melted from the wattage of his smile.

"I look forward to working with you, too," Viola said. "Have you decided on an opening date for your shop?"

"In two weeks, I plan to have a soft opening, a type of open house. You'll be one of the first to know."

Tillie Doyle didn't wait for him to offer a hand but held hers out first. "Mr. DeLuc, I adore your crepes," she gushed. "I hope I'll get an invitation to the grand opening."

"Ms. Doyle, the event would be a total failure if you weren't there."

His smile wattage went a little higher when he took Sadie's hand and held on to it a little longer. "Ms. Prince, please be sure to come. I'd be very disappointed if you couldn't make it."

"Oh, I'll be there," she stammered when he slowly withdrew his hand.

The women were absolutely spellbound by his over-the-top, practiced charm. Elise took his arm. "Ladies, I'd like to introduce Mr. DeLuc to a few more of our guests. Thank you for coming."

When they were out of earshot of the women, Elise said, "You just charmed the bloomers off the gossip queens. You should have given me a heads-up so I could have worn boots."

He chuckled lightly. "I knew what I was facing. Working on my shop, I made numerous visits to Dorrit's Diner. Those three are gossip celebrities. They could make or break my business."

"I'm going to introduce you to Madeline St. Vincent, the editor-in-chief of the *Dickens Gazette*. She's speaking with Mayor McKenzie. There are a few others, but don't worry, I won't give you a test at the end of the evening. Oh, and by the way, I like your outfit. Who are the Cosmic Jammers?"

"According to Jamie, they're a bunch of high schoolers in Eden Prairie, Indiana, who started their own band and have ten thousand followers on

YouTube. They also have an online shop for merchandise. He wants to do that for Euphoria, his band. I'm eager to hear them play."

"Giles, I can't keep up with kids these days."

"Me either. As far as the chamber music goes, I was overwhelmed and can't remember when I've seen, heard, and enjoyed a more wonderful show. Sign me up for the next performance."

"I sure will."

"Would you mind if I said hello to Matilda Cudworth?"

They paused in front of the owner of the Trim-A-Tree Shop, who had just finished talking to Amy and Andy Dorrit.

"So happy to see you, Mr. DeLuc," Matilda said. "How did you enjoy the performance?"

"Ms. Cudworth, please call me Giles. I've never heard anyone read *'Twas the Night Before Christmas* so eloquently. Your performance made the show that much more enjoyable."

"You're a real charmer, but thank you very much. Your crepes are delicious. I'll definitely be stopping by your shop. Please excuse me. I have to speak to the mayor about the tree-lighting ceremony."

"Who is next?" Giles asked Elise.

"Madeline St. Vincent."

After making the introductions, Elise took a step back and left Giles alone with the editor. Whether he wore a T-shirt from a teenage rock band or a luxurious leather jacket, he exuded confidence and style.

If anything, he knew how to work the room. Amy and Andy Dorrit joined the conversation, and it appeared they bonded quickly. Whatever he'd done in his previous job, he knew how to be cordial. He smoothly mingled with the "in crowd," and the honey just dripped off his tongue. And yet, he'd dried dishes for her, helped Emile collect garbage, and assisted Jamie with his flat tire.

Elise didn't know what to make of him. As people started to leave, she glanced at the dessert table. Only a few treats remained, but all of the crumpets and crepes had been eaten.

"That was a very advantageous introduction," Giles said, approaching her. "Madeline wants to do an article about Creperie de Dickens. I hope you don't think I came here to solicit free advertising."

"I initiated the introductions, so consider it my idea," she said.

Axel and Sebastian approached them. Both were smiling.

"Thanks for contributing the crepes. They were a big hit." Axel said.

"It was my pleasure. You two have started something great here."

"We have, but Elise runs the center and makes things happen." Sebastian put his fingertips on Elise's arm. "Emile is riding with Jamie since you all have to be at my house for Jens's birthday party."

"I'll stay and help clean up," Axel said.

"I don't have anything else to do before the party, so I'll help Elise," Giles volunteered.

"That would work," Axel said. "Freja is cooking, and I'll give her a hand. The girls are already hanging out with Lynnie and Sophie."

"See you guys later. Five o'clock," Sebastian reminded them on the way out.

"You didn't have to help, but thank you," Elise said to Giles. "Working together, we can finish sooner. Then I can give you a quick tour of the depot. There's a small kitchen down the hall. Since the cups and saucers are delicate, they will have to be washed by hand."

He wiggled his fingers. "I'm becoming an expert at helping to wash and dry dishes."

Giles finished wrapping the soft cloth around the last saucer and added it to the crate filled with delicate china. He'd learned at a very young age how to wash dishes in a commercial kitchen. His grandfather had said he had to learn the business from the ground up—starting with washing dishes and taking out the trash. The joke had been that his grandfather wanted to teach him and his brother how to make French cuisine, and his grandmother had wanted to teach them how to cook Italian. He'd learned from both worlds. Looking back, he remembered those times as simple and fun.

The past few days had brought so many changes in his life, and the most unexpected were Elise Charrette and her children. He'd never expected to be drawn so quickly into their lives, but he enjoyed their company—simple pleasures. She was personable, sweet, thoughtful, a wonderful mother, and smart…

Stop thinking in circles and avoiding the truth. She's quite lovely, and her smile is reflected in her eyes.

He didn't want to think about what would happen when she found out why he'd moved to Dickens.

"I didn't mean to be away so long," Elise said, walking into the kitchen. "When I brought the rest of the treats to Shawn, he wanted to confirm the placement of the holiday lights."

"You mean for the secret Charles Dickens visit?"

"The one we can't talk about." She looked around the small workspace. "You've packed up all of the cups and cleaned the sink. Thanks so much. All I have to do is put the crates in the back of my car."

"Do we still have time for a tour of the depot?"

She looked at her watch. "It's four. We'll take an hour, and then we'll head for Sebastian's. What did you do with your jacket?"

"Your son was kind enough to put my sweater and leather jacket in your office."

"That's where my coat is. Shawn left already, so I'll lock up on our way out. We'll go out the side entrance. It's a shorter distance to walk up the hill."

The cold air smacked them in the face when they stepped outside and took the snow-cleared path toward the depot. The late afternoon sun provided enough light to see where they were going. He was tempted to slip his glove-covered hand into hers, but he hadn't earned the right or the privilege.

The depot was right in front of them, with two large storage buildings set back. He didn't see the mini train cars. One thing that stood out was the gazebo at the curve of the tracks. He also noted white frames in the shapes of carolers, angels, snowmen, *Nutcracker*-like soldiers, and reindeer pulling Santa's sleigh.

"I take it those are the holiday lights. What's all the fuss about?"

"What you can't see is the rest of the tracks. You're looking at about a half-mile round trip. The ride takes you through a winter wonderland of lights on either side of the tracks. We've got the Nativity and a menorah. At one point, you'll ride through an archway of lights. The entire gazebo is lighted."

"That sounds amazing."

"The town's Historical Society is giving Axel and Sebastian a hard time, claiming it's too commercial and that we've lost the 'historical' element of the depot."

They paused in front of an old wood-framed building that had stood the test of time. The foundation was solid stone with seasoned brown-wood siding. A wide overhang shielded passengers from the rain or snow while waiting for the train. Three green metal benches rested on the brick platform.

"How long has this building been here?"

"Axel did extensive research on the area, but we haven't uncovered historical data on when the depot itself was built. By 1875, over a hundred different railroad companies had built rail lines, but these smaller railroads were consolidated by the larger Boston, Maine, and New Haven railroads. The tracks that serviced this area belonged to one of those smaller companies.

"He found old photos in the former milk room just off the area where the train club is set up. The construction materials for the bank barn were transported by rail car. Another photo shows the partial framework of the barn. There is a stone marker with the year 1840."

"Why does the Historical Society have a problem with this building?"

"Good question. This is where we have kids' birthday parties. The children are given a train ride. The birthday child gets a conductor's hat, and the others get trainman's caps. At the end of the ride, we read a story about American railroader Casey Jones. The parents supply the treats."

They stepped into what might have been the room for travelers waiting for the train. Wood benches had been pushed against the wall. The ticket booth was fronted by a colorful Tiffany panel. Wide wood planking covered the floor. An old woodstove on a brick platform occupied one corner.

"The building was in bad shape, but Axel insisted on retaining its integrity as much as possible when they did the rewiring. They added plumbing, radiant heat, and air conditioning. The wood-paneled walls and tin ceiling are original."

She pointed to the round glass globes suspended by a pipe. "Those are classic turn-of-the-century lights. We added the ceiling fans, but I think the bamboolike blades retain the vintage look."

He stepped closer to the walls, which were painted a dark mustard gold, and studied the black-and-white photos and pencil drawings of locomotives and travelers standing on the landing next to the depot. Horse-drawn wagons loaded with supplies were lined up along the tracks. There were several pencil drawings of the barn and a house that had been torn down.

"These look authentic. The women's dresses appear to be the style of the early 1900s. There are carpet bags next to the gentlemen wearing derby hats. That gives you some indication of the time period."

He walked back to Elise. She looked so cute, with the knit cap framing her very pretty face. *Get your mind off her.* "Has anyone determined if the photos were taken here?"

"Axel double-checked, but no dates had been added. Too bad the artists and photographers didn't show the actual train depot to authenticate its historical value."

She opened another door. The lights in this room were quite different. Iron droplights with a clear glass chimney indicated they had once been gas-powered. The room was a little larger than the waiting room. Sections of rough wood plank flooring and original plaster walls had been replaced.

"As you can see, this part of the building is still being renovated. When complete, it will be a museum."

She pushed aside a canvas tarp shielding a section of the outer wall. "From the exterior chimney, we knew there was a fireplace, but it had been plastered over. When they were repairing sections of the original plaster walls, they kept chipping away to reveal these gorgeous blue delft tiles framing the arched fireplace. I did some research. The closest I can come up with is the aesthetic-style Bedford Park Daisy tiles designed by William De Morgan."

"I know nothing about antique tiles, so I'll take your word for it. But who would put them in a train station?"

"Good question."

"Elise, I'm impressed by all you, Axel, and Sebastian have done. It's obvious you've poured your heart and soul into making this place successful while preserving the surrounding history. I loved the chamber music show, but I can't wait to take my first ride on the mini train."

Elise tapped her bottom lip, and a twinkle filled her eyes.

"You're giving me the I've-got-an-idea look," he said with a chuckle.

"You're a resident interested in the area's history. You'd love to become a member of the Historical Society."

He chuckled again in understanding. "You need my support, which I'll be happy to give, but on one condition."

She took a step back and wrapped her arms around her waist. "What?"

The hesitation and distrust in her voice were obvious. "While I was helping Jamie change his tire, he bragged about the snowman-making contest. He said his band, Euphoria, won last year. They attached brushes to the stick arms to settle atop a snare drum and added battery-powered lights and their own music. I asked if that was going to the extreme. He said absolutely not. Everyone designs a snowman, thinking outside the box. The competition is stiff but a lot of fun. Axel came in second place. Are you planning to have an entry for the event center?"

"Neither Axel nor Sebastian have said anything to me," Elise answered.

"Good. Would you, Sophie, and Emile be on my team?"

She visibly relaxed and lowered her arms. "Of course! The kids will be thrilled. Have you thought of a theme?"

"Our snowperson can wear a beret rather than a typical top hat. We'll set up an easel, and he can be painting. Maybe we can get Emile to do an original graphic drawing of a snowman making crepes. That way, people can see how talented he is."

He'd never expected to see tears sliding down her cheeks. He pulled one of his gloves from his pocket and dabbed at the wetness. "Sorry, I didn't mean to make you cry."

She sniffed. "These are happy tears. You're so kind and always thinking of others." She reached up and brushed his cheek with a little kiss. "We're going to take things up a notch. We'll balance a stack of crepes on the snowman's head with a slight tilt, like the Leaning Tower of Pisa."

"I love the idea!"

"We're also going to make a couple hundred of those crepes you made for the tea. Sophie and her friends can wear berets and pass them out, courtesy of Creperie de Dickens."

Without thinking, he pulled her into his arms and danced her around in a little circle, followed by a quick kiss. "We're going to give Jamie and his band a real challenge."

He lowered his arms, realizing too late that the spontaneity of his actions might have been too much, too familiar. "Jeez, I'm sorry, Elise. I hope I didn't offend you."

She pressed the tips of her fingers to her lips. "You didn't offend me. I kissed you on the cheek, but your aim was off. That's okay."

"Will you be offended if my aim is off some other time?"

She zipped her jacket, pulled on her gloves, and winked. "No."

"I'll definitely throw away my body GPS. Let's go to the birthday party. I'll follow you."

Chapter 5

Giles adjusted the heat spewing from the vents in his SUV. There wasn't much traffic on the country road heading into Dickens. Elise's car was right in front of him. The time he'd spent with his lovely neighbor had been so enjoyable. He'd been himself. That's the way it had been since he'd moved to Dickens. He might have gone too far with that kiss. Happiness had bubbled up inside him, and she'd been there, laughing and smiling with him. Her lips had been so soft. He'd wanted to linger, but…

Over the years, it had become too easy to flip an inner switch and become the professional who oversaw a corporation, turned up the charm to schmooze representatives from the media to give his restaurants favorable reviews, and placated a dissatisfied customer who manipulated the system by complaining to get his five-star meal compensated. Had that been manipulative? Absolutely.

Elise had told him he was kind and always thinking of others. He'd almost winced. That hadn't always been the case. An inner drive had fed his ladder to success, and sometimes, he'd pushed others out of the way.

Looking back, he didn't see a nice person. He'd been too busy overseeing his and his brother's restaurants to visit Ronald, his only sibling, who'd been taken care of by round-the-clock nurses.

Ronald's wife, Carole, had seen her husband's illness as an opportunity to oversee his brother's responsibilities, but Giles purposely avoided her company. She reminded him of a woman he'd been involved with while attending culinary school. Bess had been a user, and he'd found out almost too late.

Months before his death, Ronald had reached out to Giles for a private one-on-one. Giles had met with him in the garden behind his mansion. Not having seen his brother in months, Giles had been shaken by his brother's sickly pallor and how much weight he'd lost. He needed oxygen twenty-four hours a day. Guilt still lay heavy on Giles's heart.

On the table in front of Ron had been photos of them as young boys, working with their grandparents in their restaurant's kitchen. They wore oversized white bib aprons. Smiles filled their faces. Other photos were of them cleaning off tables and talking with loyal customers who came in week after week. That one restaurant had created a family atmosphere. Ron had made him see they'd lost touch with the simpler things. Life wasn't about money or prestige but connecting with people.

Then, his brother threw a sheaf of papers in front of Giles, making him aware of the consequences of wanting and taking too much and the repercussions others suffered due to selfishness and greed. A few months later, his only family passed on.

He missed Ron so much.

He'd gotten a call last year from Axel, who'd asked about his association with Bess Palmer and the possibility of him being a grandfather. Learning that his friend Jens had been going out with Bess at the same time he had all those years ago had been an eye-opener. His relationship with Bess hadn't been platonic, but they'd always been careful. At the time, he'd been certain he'd never fathered a child with her, but then he'd begun to question his actions.

That's when he knew he'd hit rock bottom. Walking away hadn't been easy, but he'd decided a change in life was needed before he wound up a coldhearted degenerate.

Severing ties with his former sister-in-law hadn't been a hardship. She'd gotten what she'd always wanted—she now ran the restaurant empire he and his brother had created.

Since moving to Dickens, he'd never been happier, but his growing feelings for Elise Charrette would complicate things. He'd never had the opportunity to interact regularly with kids, but he enjoyed spending time with Sophie and Emile.

Elise turned onto Main Street, Giles followed, and everything came alive. Holiday lights in front of the stores created a winter wonderland. All the parking spots along the curbs were filled, and it appeared the stores were accommodating visitors who wanted to get their holiday shopping done early.

They made a right turn down a residential street, and the holiday light show continued with already decorated homes. Some were elaborate with blow-up figurines, but others were tasteful, with strings of white lights encircling the decorative bushes and evergreen trees.

It made him aware that he had to decorate the front of his house, something he had never done before since he'd lived in a high-rise. He'd never been home and had been too busy to put up a tree or decorations. His mental checklist was growing—purchase and decorate the tree for his creperie, decorate the front of his house, get a tree for the inside. He needed an army of elves.

He parked his SUV in front of a beautiful two-story home with a signature gabled roof and wraparound porch lit with white lights. Lynnie's blow-up figurines included a huge Grinch, his dog, and a sleigh full of toys.

He glanced across the street at the house he knew Axel and Freja lived in, having visited their home last year. In front of the huge evergreen, wrapped in thousands of colored lights, was a replica of an old-fashioned steam engine with a caboose filled with gifts. On the opposite side of the walk, Holly and Ivy's choice of decorations were three blow-up figures: Santa, Frosty, and Rudolph.

He reached into the back seat for Jens's birthday present. Hopefully, they could get past the awkward stage and become good friends.

Elise greeted him with a smile. In her gloved hand was a gift bag. "Get ready for the stampede."

"Stampede?"

"Four giggly girls filled with the holiday spirit, a year-old baby who found his walking legs, and three teenagers, one of whom is Jamie's girlfriend."

Sebastian opened the Victorian-style door. "Perfect timing."

They stepped into the enclosed porch and were immediately enveloped in warmth. Bing Crosby could be heard singing "White Christmas."

"Give me your coats," Sebastian said. "I'll hang them in the hall closet."

"Something smells delicious," Giles said, passing his and Elise's coats to their host.

"Karla is just carving the turkey. She asked what Jens wanted for his birthday celebration. His favorite meal is a Thanksgiving dinner. You're in for a special treat. The brothers brought Dansk lagkage for Jens's birthday cake."

They entered a parlor in warm colors of gold and soft green. Festive decorative pillows with holiday prints decorated the cream-colored couch and two armchairs. A wood fire blazed in the brick hearth, which was covered by glass doors. Gold and silver pinecones were nestled in a thick garland illuminated by tiny white lights. Fronting the three windows was a beautifully decorated tree with hundreds of white lights. The fresh pine scent let Giles know it was quite real.

"When did you find time to put up all your decorations?" he asked.

"The tradition in this house is we decorate the weekend after Thanksgiving, even if it's the last few days of November. We got the tree yesterday from Gridley's. I'm going to be very busy with rehearsals for the holiday shows at the high school, so we wanted to keep ahead of the decorations. Karla will be putting in extra time at 2 Sisters Kringle and Fudge, too."

"Where is everyone?" Giles asked.

"We recently added a family room off the kitchen and dining room so we can monitor things, especially since Ethan has found his legs. He's into everything. Axel is in the band studio over the garage, going over some music with Jamie and his girlfriend, Ashley. Emile is with them."

"Let me see if I can help with dinner," Elise said, hurrying into the kitchen.

A loud crash coming from upstairs drew their attention. "That didn't sound good," Sebastian said. "Let me check on the Full of Mischief Four. The birthday boy is in the family room."

Double French doors opened to the huge room. In the center of the back wall was a gas fireplace with Palladian windows on either side. One corner of the room had been set up as a play area for Ethan, who was sound asleep in a soft-sided playpen.

Another wall housed a flat-screen television. Giles's old friends Lars and Jens Jorgensen were relaxing in the two recliners that were part of a sectional couch.

When he came to Dickens last year, Giles learned that the brothers owned a pastry shop in Detroit, Michigan. When the neighborhood changed, they decided to close the shop and accept Freja's invitation to work at 2 Sisters Kringle and Fudge. They'd added their own specialty pastries to Freja's list of sweet treats that could be purchased at the shop or ordered online.

The brothers, who were in their forties, had large builds that made them look like Vikings. Each had long blond hair that reached the middle of his back and was gathered by a leather tie at the base of his neck. Their deep-blue eyes were another sign of their Viking heritage. Who knew that the large hands of a Norse oarsman could make the most delicate pastry?

Both wore black wool sweaters and dark gray dress slacks with narrow cuffs. Their oxblood loafers, with little tassels, bore a shine. Lars's gold chain necklace supported a large oval coin, and Jens's supported a gold cross. They'd always dressed a step above the rest of their fellow culinary school students.

Giles was eager to renew their friendships, but he could not avoid what he was facing. "I was told this is where I'd find the birthday boy." He remembered to keep his voice low so as not to wake the baby.

Jens's blue eyes opened wide, and his face filled with a surprised smile. "Sebastian told us we were getting a surprise guest!"

"Giles!" Lars greeted, rising from the recliner.

Giles went to reach out to each man but found himself gathered in their beefy arms. Neither was gentle in his hold.

"I'm happy to see you guys and help Jens celebrate his birthday," he said, holding out the gift bag.

"Thank you, but you just being here is my gift."

Warm acceptance by his old friends was a much-welcome gift. "I need to get this out so we can get past what happened last year."

"You don't have to," Lars said. "What's in the past needs to stay in the past."

"No. I do. I had no idea Bess was going out with Jens and me at the same time or how she was using both of us. I should have taken steps to prove I hadn't fathered her daughter. For that, I apologize."

"Apology accepted. No hard feelings?" Jens asked.

"Absolutely not. I'm thrilled you're Holly and Ivy's grandfather and that Lars is their uncle." He shrugged a shoulder. "Maybe I'm a little envious since I don't have a family, but that's my loss. I've learned that friendships are important and should be appreciated. I hope we can still be friends."

Once again, he found himself wrapped up in his friends' arms. They sat in the recliners, and he made himself comfortable on the couch. He avoided talking about his life before he'd come to Dickens, so instead, he told them about Creperie de Dickens. They were thrilled and offered to help in any way.

Sebastian came into the room a few minutes later and sat on the couch next to Giles. He expelled a heavy sigh. "The girls were doing cartwheels and knocked over the chair to Lynnie's desk, which just happened to hold the manicure case with all the stuff to do their nails—with an open lid. I waited until they got everything cleaned up."

Lars chuckled. "Those girls have brought so much happiness into our lives. We love it when they visit us while we're working." To Giles, he said, "We're teaching them how to make kringle. It's important that we pass along the family traditions. Sophie fits right in with them."

It's important that we pass along family traditions. His friend's statement was a sad realization that he didn't have a family to whom he could pass on his traditions. "I haven't spent time with the four of them, but Sophie and Emile live next door to me, and I enjoy their company."

Karla came into the room, wiping her hands on a towel. The front of her red and black plaid apron, which covered her Christmas green knit shirt and jeans, read, "Santa, please stop here." She leaned down and hugged Giles quickly. "I'm so glad you could join us this evening."

She went right over to check on the baby. "He's exhausted from getting all the extra attention. Dinner is ready. The four girls have their own table. Jens, you can't miss your chair since the girls tied it with glittery balloons. My apologies if any sparkles fall onto your sweater."

"I've been a grandfather for a year and am well-seasoned. They made those balloons for me, so it makes my birthday even more special."

The dining room wasn't spared from holiday decorations. A pine garland was interwoven in the gold chandelier with additional pinecones and tiny lights. In the center of the table, covered with a white linen cloth, was a Yuletide log with four tall red candles. Each place setting had a red linen napkin.

Freja took the seat to Giles's left. Hopefully, Elise would fill the seat on his other side. He saw it as a good opportunity to offer his last apology.

"Giles, I'm sorry I didn't get to say hello when you came in," Freja said. "We're so happy you could join us."

"Thanks, Freja." He remembered to keep his voice low. "I apologized to your husband, Lars, and Jens, so I need to apologize to you, too. What I did, or didn't do, last year was totally irresponsible."

She squeezed his hand. "I accept your apology, but I, too, made mistakes that almost cost me my husband's love and Jens's friendship. That same person burned your life and mine." Freja swept a hand. "We're all sitting at the same table celebrating a dear friend's birthday, and you're here now, too. That says and means a lot."

His friend's acceptance of his apology and forgiveness of his actions were humbling. He lowered his head. "Freja, I don't know what to say other than thank you. As I said to Lars and Jens, friendships are precious and must be appreciated."

"Good enough, but you owe me," she teased.

"Name it."

"Axel couldn't stop raving about your mini orange-flavored crepes with the drizzled chocolate."

"I'll be happy to make you a batch."

He felt like the weight of the world had been lifted off his shoulders with this last apology.

Everyone seemed to converge on the table at once. Axel and the teenagers trudged in, followed by the girls running down the stairs and taking their seats at the table. Giles was happy that Elise sat in the chair next to him.

Once everyone was settled, Jens stood. "I'd like to say something. I can't tell you what it means to me and Lars to be able to celebrate my birthday with our family and friends. Holly and Ivy have filled the emptiness in our hearts with a family. As they say, the rest of you are icing on the cake."

Tears filled his friend's eyes and spilled down his cheeks. He picked up a red napkin to dab at them.

"*Bedstefar*, you're not supposed to cry on your birthday," Ivy said.

"These are happy tears, *barnebarn*."

Giles reached for his glass of iced tea and held it up. "Hear, hear! Everyone, raise your glass. We're very lucky to have you in our lives, and we wish you, Jens, the happiest of birthdays!"

"That was very nice of you," Elise said quietly. "He was really choked up."

"I've attended dinners where the main speaker choked up, and a distraction was needed." Giles realized what his statement had implied. Hopefully, she wouldn't give it much thought.

Everyone enjoyed the delicious turkey, stuffing, sweet potatoes, green bean casserole—which Giles had never cared for—honey-glazed carrots, and cornbread pudding. As a chef, he could appreciate the hard work that had gone into preparing the meal.

With this large gathering, he'd expected everyone to be talking across the table, but appetites took precedence over conversation. He also noted there wasn't a cell phone in sight. Emile sat next to Jamie and Ashley, and they talked quietly. Sebastion got up twice, and Karla followed, checking on the still-sleeping baby.

Elise kept an eye on the girls' table. They giggled and chatted while they ate. To avoid confusion, the moms had filled their plates before they'd sat down.

It occurred to him that, in reality, he was the odd man out. He didn't have a family. No, he wasn't Robinson Crusoe on an island all alone, so he'd take comfort in knowing he was sitting at a table with good friends.

Ethan woke up just as they were finishing dinner, and Karla put him in his highchair at the table to eat. Giles, having never been a parent, was surprised that she gave him adult food in moderation.

Everyone finished eating, and Elise and Freja served the coffee.

"Who's ready for birthday cake?" Karla asked as she set it in front of the birthday boy. Jens was turning forty-nine, and Karla had put that many candles on his cake.

The girls all squealed, "We are!"

"This *bedstefar* needs help to blow out my birthday candles."

Four eager volunteers gathered around his chair.

Giles was full from dinner, but the cake was a treat he couldn't pass up. Without being too obvious, he counted seven layers of vanilla cake, homemade pastry cream, and raspberry jam covered in vanilla buttercream frosting. The words *light and delicious* perfectly described the dessert.

"This is delicious," he said, wiping his mouth with the birthday napkin.

"Dansk lagkage is a traditional Danish cake. It's a little labor-intensive, but it's the perfect cake to celebrate one's birthday," Lars said.

"I'm full," Lynnie announced. "Thanks for the dinner and the cake."

The three other girls then said, "Me, too," before they all picked up their empty paper plates and walked into the kitchen. Four sets of feet hurried up the stairs.

The teenagers announced they had to check out a YouTube video and went up to Jamie's room.

Giles was in awe of what had happened. Smoothly orchestrated movements had the kids escape the room so they wouldn't be subjected to boring adult conversation. Clever kids.

"That's my cue, too," Karla said. Ethan snuggled his head against his mother's shoulder. "This one needs a bath before bedtime."

"Do you want me to give you a hand?" Sebastian offered.

She leaned in and kissed him. "Thanks, but enjoy our company."

Elise poured another round of coffee for the adults.

"So, how do you like living in the small, quiet town of Dickens?" Freja asked Giles.

"Small, quiet town?" He laughed. "There's so much activity going on, I'm afraid I'm going to miss something. Plus, I've got the Grinch house with no decorations and have to get a tree."

"The best place to go is Gridley's Farm," Lars suggested. "We took the girls to the petting zoo, and it was so much fun. Bring lots of change for the feeders, which are filled with corn to give to the critters."

"They have the official tree lighting in the square the second weekend of the month," Freja said. "That will officially start the holiday traditions and celebrations. Right after the tree lighting, they have a snowman-making contest."

"Jamie told me his band won last year." He looked at Elise and winked. "I'm going to enter the contest. Elise and the kids volunteered to help."

"What's your theme?" Axel asked.

"We're keeping it a secret," Elise answered.

"It sounds like I'm going to have to up my game for the snowman for Planes, Trains, and Automobiles."

"When do you plan to open the creperie?" Sebastian asked.

"I'm planning an open house on the Monday night after the tree lighting ceremony. It will be by invitation only. Opening to the public on the Wednesday after that. Right now, my hours will be from eleven thirty a.m. to two thirty in the afternoon. I will open again at four and close at seven-thirty on Tuesday through Saturday. I've already hired two servers and an assistant pastry chef. The dining area is all set up, except for the Christmas tree in the front window."

"When do you plan to put it up?" Lars asked.

"I'm picking up the tree and decorations from Trim-A-Tree Shop tomorrow morning, so I'll be putting it up tomorrow afternoon."

"Jens and I are finished at the bakery by three. How about we give you a hand? We can set it up between the three of us. Then maybe we can go for pizza."

"I'd be forever grateful. The pizza is on me."

Jens checked his watch. "Sorry to break up this party, but we have to be at the bakery bright and early. Thank you for making this the best birthday ever. We'll say good night to the kids and then head home."

"Let me get your coats," Sebastian offered.

"No. Sit. We're not guests but family. Giles, see you tomorrow."

Giles sipped some of his coffee, realizing his army of elves was no longer wishful thinking.

"Elise gave me a tour of the depot today, and I'm overwhelmed with what you all accomplished in a year. The history of the area is fascinating."

"I also shared our plans for Dickens Holiday of Lights, but I swore him to secrecy."

"You know they're going to ask about it Tuesday night," Freja reminded them. "Viola Hughes has let it be known she isn't an advocate for this light show. Last year, her petty gossip and misinformation almost ruined my husband's reputation and our plans for the event center. She was called out and was quiet for a while. Now she's out for revenge."

"How are you going to power the lights?" Giles asked.

"I consulted with the electronic techs at Chimera, my family's company, before we made any decisions. They're solar-powered and are on timers,"

Axel said. "This gave us freedom to put the lights in the middle of nowhere along the tracks."

"So basically, they'll have their own power source. I think that's brilliant. Before you make the suggestion, I already mentioned to Elise that I plan to join the Dickens Historical Society. You're going to need my support. When's the next meeting?"

"Tuesday night at the library annex," Freja told him.

"Should I bring some of my mini crepes as a bribe?"

"Absolutely," Freja said. "It will be our official holiday gathering."

Elise glanced at the time. "We have to get going. Tomorrow's a school day."

"I'll say good night, too," Giles said.

Once again, he followed Elise home. He flashed his lights when she pulled her car into her detached garage but hesitated before pulling into his own garage. There weren't many houses nearby, but a few had put out holiday displays. He wondered when Elise was going to put up her outside decorations.

He'd always taken the easy way out. Professionals had decorated the interior and exterior of the restaurants, but that wasn't an option around here. This was Dickens—go big or go home. They certainly had enough room in the front of their houses. He'd ask her if she had a theme in mind.

He pulled into the garage, got out of the car, and pushed the button to close the door, but a meow from the corner drew his attention. Simone had made herself comfortable on the pile of quilted covers used by the moving company.

"How did you get in here?" he asked, cradling the cat in his arms. She purred and brushed her nose against his coat. "If you like to sneak over here, I better put out food and water for you."

With Simone cradled in his arms, he reopened the garage door and headed for Elise's house. He pressed the bell, and she opened the door.

"Thank you!" she said with a sigh, immediately taking the cat from him.

"Sophie is upstairs crying her heart out, thinking the cat ran off." She turned away from Giles and hollered up the stairs. "Simone is home!"

The heartsick little girl came running down the stairs and swaddled the cat in her arms. "Simone, I thought I'd never see you again." Sophie pressed her cheek against Gile's cold coat. "Thanks for bringing her home. Mr. Giles, you're my hero."

He put his arms around the girl and the cat. "You need to have a chat with Simone about running off."

"Take her upstairs and get into bed," Elise told her daughter.

"I found her in my garage," Giles said. "The only thing I can think of is she snuck in there while the garage door was open. I plan to put out a bowl of food and water in case she decides to visit me again."

"Thank you for a wonderful day. If I can spare some time tomorrow, I'll stop by to help you decorate your tree and the front of the shop."

"That would be great."

Elise looked up the stairs and took a step closer. "Good night." She leaned into him and kissed him very softly. "Oops, my aim was off."

"It seems both our inner GPS systems are a little wacky. Lucky me. Night, Elise. See you tomorrow."

Chapter 6

On Monday morning, Elise walked into Dorrit's Diner to get an order to go. One didn't need to read a newspaper to find out what was happening in Dickens. The popular eatery served wonderful food in a hometown atmosphere with lots of friendly faces.

While the shops on Main Street had a Victorian flare, Dorrit's Diner looked like an old-fashioned passenger train car that had been converted into an eatery. The hard red seats of the booths that lined the front windows were filled with people enjoying breakfast. A small Christmas tree was nestled between the condiments and the silver napkin dispenser. Each front window bore a wreath with a red bow. White lights scalloped the edge of the blue-and-white-striped awning above the door.

Many happy feet had tread on the black carpet that ran down the center of the black-and-white checkered floor. The silver pedestals of the stools at the black and gold marbled counter always bore a shine. All but three were occupied.

Elise approached the front counter, drawn to the friendly face there. Like the captain of a ship, Amy Dorrit commanded the helm. Her friend was wearing a smock decorated with snowmen and dancing Santas. The bushy end of her long white braid was decorated with a red bow. Amy was always down-to-earth and spoke her mind. Elise loved that about her friend.

"Hi, Elise. I have to tell you how much we enjoyed the show and tea yesterday. I hope you invite the group back. Maybe do a military presentation for Memorial Day or the Fourth of July."

"I'm so glad you enjoyed the show, and I love your idea of an American tribute. Earlier, I sent the musicians a message to tell them how much everyone loved the show and asked for their dates of availability. I'll offer them a contract if they have either of those holidays open."

Amy leaned closer to the counter. "The town criers were in here earlier, and the buzz was about the show yesterday but also about Giles DeLuc. According to the mouthy three, the world traveler and his creperie will add a bit of culture to the town and shoppers' experience."

"They are so full of themselves."

Three customers approached the counter to pay their checks.

"Excuse me a moment, Elise," Amy said.

While waiting, Elise checked her email. One message was from the booking agent who handled the chamber music group, with their dates of availability. She quickly responded, requesting a booking for the July Fourth weekend. As part of the show, she'd have three teenagers dressed in costume, two playing the snare drum and one playing the flute, to replicate Archibald Willard's painting The Spirit of '76, which symbolized the spirit of the American Revolution.

She'd also ask Matilda to be Betsy Ross. This time, there would be no tea and crumpet get-together afterward. They'd have a barbecue!

"I love my job," Elise announced with a happy smile when Amy returned. "I just planned the event for the Fourth of July, which includes booking the chamber music group."

"Sign me up! We were talking about Giles DeLuc."

"You mentioned the mouthy three. They're portraying him as a world traveler, a charismatic snob who will raise Dickens's culture level. I can assure you Giles is not like that. He's very down-to-earth. He didn't want to tell everyone he made those delicious crepes, not wanting to steal the thunder from our party. I'm the one who let the attendees know who made those treats."

"That tells me he's got integrity."

"I told him the same thing. Giles is joining the Dickens Historical Society and will be at the meeting tomorrow night."

"I'll be there, too, but my husband won't be able to join us. I'm anxious to hear your plans for the light show."

Thankfully, Amy had guarded her words. "We'll need your support."

Elise was just about to give her order when she heard someone call her name. She turned to see Madeline St. Vincent. The editor-in-chief of the newspaper quickly unwrapped the scarf around her neck and lowered the zipper of her puffy jacket. The knit hat on the back of her head created a halo of blond hair. The cold morning air had made her cheeks red.

"Just the person I'm looking for." Madeline shoved her gloves in her pocket.

"Good morning, Madeline."

"Yesterday's event was wonderful. I hope you plan to invite the musicians back."

"Amy and I were just discussing that. How can I help you?"

"Viola, Sadie, and Tillie reached out to me. They're my friends, but I was caught off-guard last year by not fact-checking their story's details. What can you tell me about your plans for the Dickens Holiday of Lights? According to the gossip queens, you're planning this elaborate display. The sky will be illuminated by audacious beams of light to announce a grand opening. It will draw shoppers away from town."

"Jeez. Spotlights? That's old-school," Amy tossed out with a chuckle.

Elise wanted to burst out laughing but held it in. "I appreciate you wanting to confirm the details with me first. I can assure you we have no plans for 'audacious beams of light.' We'll discuss it more at the Historical Society meeting tomorrow evening."

"Unfortunately, I won't be able to attend due to a prior commitment. I'm sure they'll fill my ear the next day with their version of what happened."

"Madeline, I'll be there and take notes," Amy said.

The woman wiggled her eyebrows at Elise. "You were quite friendly with him yesterday. Should I be reading more into your relationship?"

This kind of a rumor she didn't need. "There is no relationship other than he lives next door to me. End of story."

Madeline reached into her pocket for her gloves. "I have to run. Amy, I'll take a black coffee to go."

As soon as the woman paid for her drink, she breezed out of the dinner.

"I'd better get my breakfast before someone else asks me questions about the depot or Giles DeLuc. I'd like a bacon, egg, cheese wrap, and coffee to go. I'm on my way to help my aunt and uncle work on fudge orders."

"Coming right up."

2 Sisters was three short blocks away from the diner. Green-painted benches had been sporadically placed between storefronts. Despite the cold, Elise sat down to enjoy her wrap and coffee and take in her surroundings.

A fresh pine garland framed the doors of businesses with red bows and white lights. Flower boxes spaced close to the curb sprouted pine branches, large white pinecones, and red and green ornaments. Solar-powered white lights were scattered throughout the branches.

The Christmas music from the public speakers mounted atop the Victorian streetlights decorated with fresh wreaths drifted throughout the shopping area. The park, with a beautiful gazebo, was at the very end of Main Street. That's where they would be holding the snowman-making contest after the tree lighting.

She raised her face to capture the warmth of the sun on her cheeks. Who would have thought a year ago that she'd be sitting on a bench now, surrounded by festive decorations that replicated a Currier & Ives Christmas card? More than ever, she was convinced relocating here had been the right decision.

She finished her wrap and coffee and threw the empty cup and foil into a garbage receptacle. Her slow walk to 2 Sisters took her past Giles's shop. All was dark inside. She liked him very much and wanted to know so much about him, but asking questions about his life before he'd come here might be an invitation for him to ask about her past.

A few minutes later, she reached her destination. The joyful feeling she experienced stepping into the fudge and kringle shop never got old. She was immediately enveloped in sugary sweetness and happiness.

Three long glass display cases afforded a perfect view of the variety of fudge the shop sold. One case held holiday flavors and shapes—reindeer, green pine trees, white fudge snowflakes, candy canes, and red Santas.

In the center of the room was a circular display of small white boxes with a variety of preweighed fudge to make purchases more convenient. Many customers wanted to sample different flavors before purchasing, so the shop offered precut samples in tiny cups.

A glass-fronted case on the other side of the shop displayed an assortment of kringle and select pastries. Elise knew they would sell out by noon unless customers preordered.

Her Aunt Britta was responding to a customer's inquiry about the distinction between chocolate and fudge flavors.

"Our unique holiday-shaped cutouts may resemble chocolate, but they're our 2 Sisters Kringle and Fudge trademark fudge. Chocolate is a mix of cocoa solids, cocoa butter, sugar, and other flavorings. It's hard and solid. Our fudge is a mixture of sugar, dairy, and flavorings cooked and cooled to form a smooth, semisoft confection."

"Those candy canes look wonderful," the customer said. "I'll take twelve, a dozen Christmas trees, and a dozen snowmen. Oh, and a cherry kringle and six of the Stollen pastries."

Her Uncle Dane used a knife to cut into a slab of white fudge mixed with chopped Oreos for the customer he was waiting on. Then, he moved to the scale to weigh the purchase. He also helped a customer with a selection of dark chocolate fudge.

Her aunt and uncle had turned sixty a few months ago. Both wore candy-cane-striped vests over their white shirts. Aunt Britta had added a sprig of artificial holly to her white-blond hair, which she wore in short waves. Uncle Dane's formerly dark brown hair was sprinkled with a generous helping of gray hair. Even when he wasn't working, he favored bow ties. The one he was wearing was red.

Her mother's sister and her husband had never let the distance between their homes prevent them from being a close-knit family. They'd visited each other at their home in Atlanta or come to Chicago three or four times a year.

They had managed a fudge and candy shop in Atlanta. A number of years ago, they visited Dickens and fell in love with the quaint town. When the business in Atlanta was sold, they moved to Dickens.

The bell over the door tinkled, indicating a customer had just left.

"Here's our princess in shining armor. Come to help us fill fudge orders," Uncle Dane teased before taking a drink from the insulated bottle he kept behind the counter.

Aunt Britta quickly hugged Elise. "How's my favorite niece?"

"You only have one. Princess in shining armor? Really, Uncle Dane."

"We appreciate you helping us out. How are my babies?"

As her aunt and uncle had never had any children of their own, Sophie and Emile were looked upon as their grandchildren. "They're fine and look forward to all the fun activities in Dickens."

"Before you go home, make sure you take them some fudge," Dane said.

"I will, Uncle Dane."

Britta drank from her own insulated mug. "Come on back to the warehouse. We've got two hundred orders to fill and get in the mail by tomorrow. And this is only the beginning of the holiday season."

"That's a lot of orders. Who will work the front of the shop with Uncle Dane?"

"Since no busloads of tourists are scheduled until tomorrow, Dane won't have any problem working alone. We hired three part-timers to help during the Christmas holidays since we'll be open until nine o'clock. They're high school friends of Jamie and Ashley."

Elise and Britta stepped into the kitchen, where Lars and Jens were busy making kringle. Stacked racks on wheels were filled with freshly baked kringle. The smell was heavenly. They were so busy she offered only a friendly wave.

"Where's Freja?"

"On her way to Boston. She's meeting with the committee hosting the National Kringle Competition."

"I know she won the competition last year. Is she entering again?"

"Oh, no. When asked about the contest, she tells everyone that she competed, won, and that's the end. This year, she's been asked to be a judge."

They passed the area in the commercial kitchen where the different flavors of fudge were made and stepped into the warehouse. Stainless steel tables lined one side of the large space. Boxes assembled for shipping fudge and pastry were neatly stacked on shelves, and stacking trays were filled with fudge.

On the other side of the warehouse, the kringle and pastry orders were made ready for shipping. They guaranteed that orders would be shipped within twenty-four hours of baking. The racks were empty but would be filled by late afternoon.

Freja and Karla's office was off to the side, where they spent very little time.

"Since Karla devised a different formula for 2 Sisters fudge so it can be colored and cut into various shapes, we've been struggling to keep up with the high demand. The variety package is also one of our biggest online sellers. The shipping labels are already on the boxes."

Elise gave her aunt a little smile of understanding. She'd helped with their overflow of Halloween orders and knew the routine. "The small white boxes with the cellophane window are for the chocolate figures. I'll find a copy of the order in the shipping box."

Britta handed Elise a pair of plastic gloves and a shower cap to put over her hair. "Board of Health rules."

She stuffed her hair under the cap and pulled on the gloves. "You've got me until three o'clock. I've already handled the stuff for the event center. Sophie has Girl Scouts at Karla's house, and Emile has special band practice after school, so I'm going to help Giles DeLuc decorate the tree he wants to put up in his shop."

"I'm sorry we didn't get to see the show yesterday since we had to work. Jamie, that sweetheart, videoed the show and sent it to your Uncle Dane. When Lars and Jens came in this morning, they couldn't stop talking about the birthday dinner. We were invited, but we had to make the fudge. They brought us a piece of birthday cake and shared the photos they took."

"I'm sorry you had to miss all the fun. Have you taken on too much work?"

"We love managing the shop and helping Karla make the fudge. The shop is closed the week between Christmas and New Year's, so we plan to relax. The sisters have been very generous and give us three weeks of vacation. After the holidays, we get a little reprieve, and then we have Valentine's Day madness."

While they talked, Elise put each fudge figurine into its individual slot and covered the confection with a puffy protective sheet. The shop's logo had been imprinted on the lid. Karla and Freja insisted on sending a personal message to their customers. Before wrapping the box with a preassembled ribbon, she enclosed a card that expressed the shop's thanks and wished the recipient a happy holiday.

Aunt Britta came in and out a few times when Uncle Dane sent a message that he needed help out front.

When she returned after a lengthier absence, Britta said, "Sorry that I haven't been pulling my load, but an unexpected busload came into town, and it seems like their first stop was this shop." She handed Elise a glass of iced tea and a Stollen Danish still warm from the oven. "Lars and Jens sent this for you."

"Not a problem, thanks." Elise had pulled up a stool and sat while she worked. She drank some of her iced tea and took a bite of the delicious pastry. "This is so yummy. I could never work here full-time. I'd gain twenty pounds."

"I work around this fudge and pastry, so I understand. Elise, be honest with me. Are you happy that you moved here and with your job?"

"You know what I was facing in Chicago. I'll be forever grateful you helped us move and got me a job that I love."

Elise reached for another white box but stopped. "Sophie told me the other night that Emile discovered that Claude had hidden bottles of wine in a closet in the basement. Emile dumped out the wine and filled them with colored water. I recognize that Claude worked hard and never had time for the kids or me. He was obsessed with opening that restaurant. I've been trying to keep a low profile, praying those crooked money lenders don't find us."

Tears escaped her eyes. Before she could wipe her cheeks, Aunt Britta brushed the tears away with a white handkerchief and drew Elise into her arms.

"I'm so sorry you've had to go through that terrible time. You're still suffering from his obsession and selfishness. You had to give up everything to protect your children. Claude had his problems, but not all men are like him."

Elise sniffed and smiled at her aunt, her best friend. "I thought I was giving up everything at the time, but it was the best decision I ever made. Living in Dickens close to you and Uncle Dane and our wonderful friends, we couldn't be happier." She pushed out of her aunt's arms. "Thanks for your shoulder cry. I can handle the rest of these. I'll let you know when I'm done."

"One question. Do you like Giles DeLuc? Really like him?"

Knowing her answer wouldn't leave the room, she could be honest with her aunt. "I do, very much. He's fun, kind – to me and the children – thoughtful, and very good-looking. We enjoy each other's company. He makes the most delicious crepes. I've never met anyone like him."

"Then open your heart."

Elise reached for another box and muttered, "How can I open my heart to a person I really like when I'm being deceitful?"

Giles jammed his hands on his hips and stared at the green puzzle on the floor, which was his Christmas tree. When he'd picked up the big box from Trim-A-Tree, he'd thought the tree would be assembled, and all he'd have to do was set it in front of the window.

He'd already shifted the tables so there would be enough space for the tree. To make matters worse, his helper elves had sent him a message that they wouldn't be there until five o'clock. They had a big baking order that had to be finished and ready for shipping tomorrow morning. They'd bring the pizza and drinks with them.

His intentions to get started with decorating had fallen by the wayside. He'd accepted a delivery of supplies and stored everything on the kitchen shelves. Then he'd made the mistake of pulling out his grandmother's old recipe book and gotten swept up in her past, considering many of the recipes were in French. She'd added personal notes about family members, such as her brother had owned a small vineyard, but she'd thought the wine tasted like colored vinegar.

He understood French, but he wasn't fluent in speaking it. Luckily, his grandmother had insisted he learn to read the basics so that he could interpret the recipes.

A knock on the front door urged him to get up off the floor. The face on the opposite side of the glass was the prettiest helper elf he'd ever seen. In her hand was a paper carrier with two cups, and in the other was an oversized carryall.

"Tell me you know how to put a Christmas tree together, and I'll make you dinner for a year," he teased, opening the door.

"I've put together a tree or two, and cooking for me won't be necessary," she returned with a little laugh. She set the cardboard holder and her bag on a nearby table and handed him a cup.

"Coffee?"

"Hot chocolate. The whipped cream has probably melted." She reached inside the carryall and removed a white bag. "Fresh chocolate chip cookies from Leslie's Bakes and More. I thought you could use a break."

"Thank you. Sit for a few minutes," he invited.

She draped her coat over the back of a chair and removed her knit cap.

He sat across from her. "I'm finding out more and more what I've taken for granted, having people do things for me because I didn't have time." He swept a hand to the parts of the tree spread out on the floor. I've never put a tree together and feel inept." He didn't bother to hide his frustration.

"Don't feel bad. I'll feel like a fish out of water when we go to Gridley's to chop down a real tree."

Giles removed the lid from the cup and took a sip of hot chocolate. He laughed a little. "Before moving to this town, I never considered having a cup of hot chocolate. This has to be Dickens's signature drink."

"You mean like a Hallmark Christmas movie?"

"Elise, you can't tell anyone, but I've never watched a Hallmark Christmas movie." He broke off a piece of an oversized cookie and drank more of his hot chocolate. The combination of warm cookies and hot chocolate was delicious.

"Don't tell Sophie or the Full of Mischief Four. They love those movies and watch their favorites over and over again."

"Maybe I should join them some night."

"They'd love that. Before we get started, how about giving me a tour?"

"You're the first one I'm sharing this with, other than the workers who painted, put down new floors, and installed the kitchen." He swept a hand. "What you see is Creperie de Dickens."

"When I first walked in, I got the feel of a casual sidewalk café. You can enjoy a leisurely lunch or a little more upscale dinner with delicious food."

"That makes me very happy since that is what I'm going for. You don't need all the fancy pomp and circumstance that, in my opinion, takes away from the quality and delicious food." It was too bad he hadn't realized that years ago.

He wasn't that person anymore.

"Don't let the owner of a five-star upscale restaurant hear you say that," she remarked. "I organized a number of dinner parties that my clients insisted be held in a fancy, swanky environment. I argued that a step down would provide better-quality food. They didn't care and wanted to impress people."

They were probably my restaurants. He looked around, smiling. "For the holidays, I'll add plain green tablecloths and red glass votive candle holders. Beverages will be a bottle of spring water on each table, but I'll also offer coffee or tea. You can thank your children for their suggestions of having ice cream with my dessert crepes. Speaking of your children, where are they?"

"Sophie is at a Girl Scout meeting at Karla's house. It will be a little longer today since they're making holiday cards for the residents at the assisted living center. Emile is at a special band practice for the holiday show at the high school. He plays the Alto Saxophone. He'll go home with Sebastian and Jamie. Karla will feed them, too. I've got till about six thirty.

"Lars and Jens are bringing pizza for dinner at five."

"Perfect. Let's get going on your tree. They can decorate the outside with lights and garland around the window and door."

"So where do we start?"

"I don't want to insult you, but did you read the instructions that came with the tree?"

"No," he said, shaking his head. "I was overwhelmed by all the branches. Now I really feel like a fool."

She patted him on the cheek. "Assembling a Christmas Tree 101." Elise picked up one of the smaller branches. "Each one is color-coded. Place the stand in the center of the front window. Let's build us a Christmas tree."

Between the two of them, they assembled the tree and got the lights working in a half hour. Hanging the ornaments took a lot longer. His helper elf insisted on spreading the branches to make the tree fuller. She oohed and aahed over the specialty ornaments that Matilda from Trim-A-Tree had ordered with the French theme. Elise was also a perfectionist when it came to putting on the gold-and-silver-beaded garland.

At five o'clock, his other helper elves arrived, carrying two pizza boxes, two bottles of soda, paper cups, and a bag of ice.

"Perfect timing. We just finished the tree," Giles told them.

"It looks beautiful. After we eat, we'll decorate the front of the store," Jens said.

Over their Italian dinner, they discussed Giles's upcoming open house the following Monday. He shared his menu with his friends and told them about his grandparents, who had influenced his dream of opening his own creperie.

The Jorgensen's reminisced about their family coming from Denmark and starting their small bakery, where the guys had learned to bake. He felt a unique camaraderie with his friends. When he got time, he'd research traditional Danish foods and create a unique crepe in honor of them.

A little after six, Elise and Giles joined Lars and Jens outside to look at the lights and garland decorations on the front of the shop.

"Wait! Let's open the vertical blinds and turn on the tree lights," Elise suggested. "We can get the total effect."

"Great idea." He didn't give any thought to what he was doing and took Elise's hand when they stood back to admire their combined efforts.

"Who said you have to go to Rockefeller Center to look at a great tree and holiday decorations? I feel like I'm looking at a Christmas card. You guys did a great job!"

"Thanks, Giles, but we enjoy decorating," Lars said. "The girls renewed our spirit of having fun during the holidays."

Giles shook hands with each of his friends. "Thanks for everything."

"You're welcome, and we've got to get going," Jens said. "We're looking forward to Monday and your great food."

Giles and Elise walked back into the shop. He still couldn't get over the transformation. He felt good, really good. Elise had covered the tables with green cloths and added short red glasses to hold votive candles. "The place looks incredible."

"I agree. Don't throw away the ornament boxes or the directions for the tree," she teased.

"Very funny."

Elise checked her watch. "I've got fifteen minutes, and then I've got to pick up my children. One thing I forgot to ask. Did you send out invitations?"

"This morning. My fifty invites include all of the shop owners, the powers that be, and the media. Since I don't have your personal email address, I sent it to the center's email."

"Good save. You're still going with us for a real Christmas tree on Saturday?"

"Are you kidding? After today, I'm an expert at putting up a tree and decorating. I might add that my Christmas elves helped a bit. I still have to get a tree skirt."

"Oh, that reminds me." Elise went to her oversized bag and pulled out a gift. "Here's something special for your tree. If you don't like it, I can return it to Trim-A-Tree."

Giles opened the gift wrapping to reveal a white tree skirt decorated with comical chefs, cooking, and baking implements.

"I realize it's comical, but I didn't think you'd want something frilly."

"I love it! Come on, help me put the finishing touch to our tree."

When it was in place, he turned to her and slipped a casual arm around her waist. "Now it's perfect. You've made my first time decorating so special. I'd really like to kiss you. Nod, if it's okay."

He was disappointed when she didn't nod, but she surprised him by putting a hand on his cheek and kissing him first. He pulled her closer, enjoying the taste of her sweet lips and the feel of her soft, womanly body.

"This time, my aim was right on target," she breathlessly confessed before tapping him on the chest. "Now I have to get going."

He needed to catch his breath, wishing their shared kiss hadn't ended so soon. "What time is the Historical Society meeting at the library annex tomorrow night, and do you want to ride together?"

"It starts at seven and ends by eight-thirty, but I'd like to leave around six. It's our regular meeting, but it will be our holiday get-together. I'm helping Karla set out the coffee and desserts. We'd be happy to ride with you. Jamie and Ashley will be watching the kids in the children's center."

His cell phone pinged with an incoming text. He hoped it was from his friend who owned the art gallery. It wasn't, and he made the mistake of reading the message.

Have you cleaned up the mess, and are you ready to get back to work? Write a check and get her out of your system.

Temper soaring, he quickly deleted the message.

"Is everything all right?"

"The company I was associated with wants some advice on an account," he lied. "They can wait. Thanks again. See you tomorrow night."

His temper still hadn't subsided from his former sister-in-law's message. It had been a year, and she still hadn't accepted that he'd stepped away from his former life and her.

Chapter 7

"Since I'm about to become a member of the Dickens Historical Society, what can you tell me about the library annex?" Giles asked Karla, the group's current president. Elise was in the small kitchen off of the room, making coffee.

A guest podium fronted two rows of folding chairs he had just finished setting up. They'd covered the dessert table with a red plastic tablecloth. Karla had reused one of the centerpieces from the tea at the event center. Clear plastic wrap covered oval platters of kringle, Danish, and his mini crepes. He laughed to himself. There were no delicate china dishes or fancy linens this evening. He'd set out the paper cups, red and green paper napkins, and plastic utensils.

Karla placed a yellow pad on top of the podium. "That's very nice of you to ask since this place is special to Freja and me. Our Great-Great-Grandfather Nohr Sorensen, our *bedstefar*—that's *grandfather* in Danish—was the first pastor here. The church was built in 1870. I found documentation in the church archives that indicated there are several graves below the original foundation."

"Are you saying it's haunted?"

Karla gave him a little smile. “I haven’t come face-to-face with my *bedstefar*, but I truly believe he’s still around.”

“I’ve never encountered a ghost and will take your word for it.”

“When the bishop deconsecrated the church, our late father was on the town council and petitioned the town to turn it into a library annex, hoping to keep the original stone building from being demolished. The town allows us to use the finished rooms here in the basement to hold monthly club meetings.”

Karla rested her arms on the podium. “Three years ago, I decided to restore the original bells that were forged in 1860. From reading some of my grandmother’s notes, the bells would ring on Christmas Eve and could be heard throughout the countryside. I didn’t anticipate the additional costs to repair the rotted condition of the original framework. I got much pushback from three members for what they called an ‘excessive, frivolous’ proposal and who were dead set against my project.”

He held up a hand. “I know who you mean. Viola Hughes, Sadie Prince, and Tillie Doyle. I only just met them and realized their mission in life is to be argumentative and annoying.”

Elise walked out of the kitchen and handed Karla and Giles paper cups that hinted at the scent of freshly brewed coffee. “I added a little half-and-half to each.”

"Thanks." He took a moment to sip coffee. "Karla explained the challenge she faced restoring the bells."

"Last year, the gossip queens spread an inflated rumor about the mini train ride, declaring Axel and Sebastian were going to build an amusement park," Elise added.

"That's not all," Karla said. "Viola gave my sister and me the hardest time when we started mail-order services for kringle and fudge. She claimed the businesses in town would suffer if customers found it easier to order online."

"So basically, you've had a continuing battle uphill," Giles said. "As far as I'm concerned, you've proven what an asset the center can be, especially after Sunday afternoon's performance. This may be a meeting of the Historical Society, but I'll bet they won't pass up the opportunity to bombard you with questions about the Dickens Holiday of Lights."

"We're expecting it, but I won't be alone," Elise said. "Axel and Sebastian will be here, too. We've come up with a plan that we hope will put a few chinks in their armor of resentment."

"I'll do my best to support you," Giles assured.

The members started coming into the room. Giles remembered the people he had met at the tea—Jillian Morgan, the florist, and Matt Mathews, who owned Dickens Hardware. He'd also met Morty from Morty's Deli.

He'd had a brief conversation with Trix Warden, who owned Dickens Art Studio. He told her about Emile's graphic arts. The owner would love to look at some of the teen's work when Emile was ready.

Matilda Cudworth had arrived with Amy Dorrit. Both mentioned to Giles that they'd gotten their invitations to his creperie's open house and would be attending. Matilda let him know the decorations on the front of his shop looked lovely, and she was eager to see his French-themed tree.

The women were dressed in festive red or green. The guys sported sweaters and dress slacks. Something had told him not to wear jeans, so he'd worn dress slacks and a wine-colored sweater. Axel and Sebastian arrived together and socialized with the other attendees. From what Giles could determine, the pair was well-liked.

He sat next to his friends in the second row.

"Thanks for being here, Giles," Axel said. "Freja is disappointed she couldn't come. Her flight is delayed because of an unexpected squall that swept the airport."

To Giles's relief, Elise sat next to him. He kept his voice low. "I noticed the other members avoided taking the three end chairs in the front row."

Elise lightly nudged his upper arm. "There's an invisible sign on them."

"The meeting will be starting soon. Hopefully, the trio of troublemakers got lost."

"Better yet, aliens might have kidnapped them," Elise returned.

He groaned when Viola Hughes, Sadie Prince, and Tillie Doyle walked in and sat in the vacant seats. "No such luck."

Karla stepped up to the podium. "Thanks for taking time out of your busy schedules to attend our meeting. If no one has objections, we'll dispense with reading the minutes and the treasurer's report and post them on our website. Since we're doing that, Elise has asked to present something special to the group."

"Wish me luck. I'm going to need it," she whispered to Giles.

"I won't ask why, but good luck."

Elise moved to stand behind the podium and removed the book she'd put on the lower shelf when she'd come in earlier.

"Thank you, Karla. We're all interested in history and preserving the past, or we wouldn't be here. I wanted to share a story my daughter, Sophie, is reading." She held up the book. "*The Carpenter's Gift: A Christmas Tale About the Rockefeller Center Tree*. This classic Christmas story teaches children the spirit of the season by combining two great New

York City traditions: the Rockefeller Center Christmas tree and the neighbor-helping-neighbor program of Habitat for Humanity."

"Does this mean you're going to put on a children's play at the event center like Karla did with *The Bells of St. Dickens*?" Tillie Doyle asked.

Inwardly, Elise groaned, and she'd only just started.

"Tillie," Amy said, "wait until she's finished before you start asking questions."

"Set during the Depression in New York City, *The Carpenter's Gift* tells the story of eight-year-old Henry and his father selling Christmas trees. They give a Christmas tree to construction workers building Rockefeller Center and celebrate together. Through the kindness of the construction workers and neighbors, Henry gets his wish for a nice, warm home to replace his family's drafty shack. He plants a pinecone from that first Rockefeller Center tree.

"As an old man, Henry repays the gift by donating the enormous tree that has grown from that pinecone to become a Rockefeller Center Christmas tree. After bringing joy to thousands, its wood is used to build a home for another family in need."

"That is a beautiful story," Trix Warden said. "I'd like to read the book myself."

"We have three copies in the library," Karla announced.

"Axel and Sebastian have preserved a historic barn and train station," Elise went on, "but they'd like to do something more. The Dickens Historical

Society's purpose is to preserve the past for future generations, something similar to the storyline in the book. The center will purchase young trees from Gridley's. We'll plant the saplings in the field behind the depot. Each one will be marked with a date so future generations can track their growth."

Viola harrumphed. "And I suppose *you're* going to take credit for this idea of preserving the past."

Dead silence filled the room. *Patience.* "Viola, you didn't let me finish. The acreage will display a hand-engraved sign that says Dickens Historical Evergreen Preserve. People will be invited to plant a tree. To keep uniformity, we'll cover the cost to have a plaque made with the person's name and date."

"Is this some spur-of-the-moment idea to try and schmooze the Historical Society? How do you plan to plant all these trees when the ground is frozen?" Sadie Prince challenged.

Elise's eyes darted to Sebastian with a plea for help. He nodded and stood.

"Sadie, this was not a spur-of-the-moment idea. Would you rather we sell off the extra acreage to some developer to build a factory, or would you rather we preserve the beauty of the land?"

"I didn't say that!"

He came right back, not withholding the annoyance in his voice. "It's what you implied. We've already considered the frozen ground. The center will have an Arbor Day celebration to plant the trees."

"Who is going to plant the first tree?" Viola asked in a snippy voice.

Elise wanted to scream and put gags on their mouths. Why were they being so difficult? Sebastian and Axel loved her idea, which also reflected community service.

Only one person had a skilled hand in managing these three "difficult" individuals. She gave Giles a pleading look.

He winked before standing.

"Viola, as head of the Chamber of Commerce, you should be the first one to plant a tree, setting an example for the entire community and commemorating Arbor Day. Think about the publicity it will generate. It might even go viral."

From the smile that filled her face, the woman appeared to glory in his praise. "Giles, that's a wonderful idea. I'd be honored."

Jeez, the woman's hero worship of Giles is obvious. Elise started to relax until Sadie Prince shot up from her chair and glowered at everyone.

"We're getting ahead of ourselves! Arbor Day is in April, but this is December. You're claiming that the train depot has historical value, but we only have your word, even if you found a few little tracks."

The woman should have known better than to put down Axel's pride and joy. There seemed no way to please these three. Temper radiated from him when he stood.

"Sadie, by 1875, over a hundred railroad companies had built rail lines, but the larger Boston, Maine and New Haven railroads consolidated the smaller railroads. I located the tracks, but I'm determined to locate the name of the small railroad that was used to transport the materials for the barn/event center. We plan to open the other half of the depot as a museum. Even if we proved Charles Dickens stopped at our train depot, you wouldn't be satisfied. You'd want to meet the man face-to-face!"

His piqued tone was quite obvious and accompanied by a number of gasps from the others. Before Elise or Sebastion could offer support, Tillie stood and faced the members, escalating the combustive mood in the room.

"You're planning to set up some elaborate light display that has nothing to do with history! It will draw visitors and shoppers away from Dickens. Look at all the energy you'll be wasting on some frivolous display!"

Elise curled her fingers tightly into her palms before rebutting Tillie's claim. "The lights are solar, drawing their own power from the sun. They're on timers and go off at the end of the evening."

She realized she, too, needed to calm down and drew in a deep breath. "Tillie, our intention is to make a lot of children happy," Elise went on. "It will only be for two weekends. We won't make a cent. The children will bring a toy donation to be shared with those who are less fortunate. We're continuing the spirit of giving."

"The next thing you know," Viola said, "you'll want to have that audacious light display for the Fourth of July and Halloween."

"Viola, that's a wonderful idea!" Elise said. "Think of all the business that would draw to Dickens off-season. We could display the seasonal lights in conjunction with a musical event," she added. She kept it to herself that she had already booked the event in July and the magic show in October.

"I didn't mean…" Viola sputtered.

"This isn't getting us anywhere," Karla said, taking over the meeting. "Since many of the shop owners are here, let's take a vote. Raise your hand if you think the Dickens Holiday of Lights will draw customers away from your shops."

Three hands went up—the troublemakers.'

The owner of Morty's Deli stood. "I think it will draw more visitors. I'll even name a special deli sandwich."

Matilda looked directly at Viola. "At our last Chamber of Commerce meeting, we mentioned that we wanted something fresh and new to draw more visitors, especially in the evenings. The event center is definitely drawing more visitors."

"But those lights will draw people away from town!" Viola argued.

Giles raised his hand before standing. "May I say something?"

Karla sighed with relief. "For those of you who haven't met him, this is Giles DeLuc, the owner of Creperie de Dickens."

"Thank you for accepting my membership in the Historical Society and Chamber of Commerce. Viola was kind enough to provide your email addresses so I could invite you all to my open house on Monday."

"We can't wait to taste your crepes," Matilda let everyone know.

"I've listened to both sides of your arguments," Giles continued. "It's obvious that Axel and Sebastian have proven the historical value of the event center and train depot. Their aim is to fill children's hearts with joy this holiday season. The other side is you're afraid the Dickens light show will draw shoppers away from the stores. I have an idea for something different to draw visitors into Dickens, but I have a question for Elise. What time is the Dickens Holiday of Lights? And how long is the train ride itself?"

"We were planning to start the first one around six, once it's fully dark. As for the length of the ride?" She looked at Axel.

"Twenty minutes at most," Axel said. "The last ride will leave the depot around eight-thirty."

"That's perfect," Giles nodded. "Shoppers are invited to attend a Cocoa Crawl. Starting and ending times are to be determined. Visitors are given a card listing the participating stores. They would have to go to each shop, have a cup of hot chocolate, and move on to the next. The cups don't have to be large. In order to be eligible for a grand prize, they'd have to go to every shop and have the card stamped. It's a way to get them into your stores."

"As I understand, each store would supply its own hot cocoa," Trix confirmed. "I'm sure there will be more than one person with a winning card."

"Yes. You could have a drawing of the winning cards," Giles said.

"Where would the finalists drop off their cards?" Amy asked.

"I could set up a Dropbox for the completed cards and notify the winner," Giles offered.

"This is a wonderful idea, but who would cover the cost of this grand prize?" Viola asked. "The town can't afford some outlandish giveaway!"

"I have a suggestion," Karla said. "Each participating store could contribute a small gift, which we'd put in a basket for a grand prize. If you include one of your cards, that, too, would be a reminder of where they shopped."

"Perfect," Elise said. "After they're done with the Cocoa Crawl, they could head out to the Dickens Holiday of Lights train ride. If they don't have children, they'd still come into Dickens to participate in the Cocoa Crawl since the stores will be open until nine p.m. Everyone would benefit—visitors, shoppers, and children."

"So basically, we're talking about having hot chocolate and a small prize for the basket for two weekend events," Matilda confirmed. "I love the idea."

Elise decided to imitate Giles's honey-smooth charm technique toward Viola. "As the head of the Chamber of Commerce, everyone will look to you, Viola, for confirmation and direction about this new event to draw shoppers into Dickens."

"It will be a credit to your leadership, and they might label you a hero," Giles added. "Remember, everyone wins—the store owners and the children."

"Well," Viola muttered, straightening her back. "As long as those lights are tasteful and don't waste energy. You say the ride is just for children?"

"Children must be accompanied by an adult," Sebastion answered. "That means grandparents are also eligible."

"I can't make the decision myself," Viola said, "so once again, let's have a show of hands. Is everyone agreeable to this Cocoa Crawl?"

Every hand went up. *Thank God!*

"We'll coordinate the Cocoa Crawl with the shop owners to sign up and put together the cards that will be given to the visitors to have stamped. Send the information to my assistant so that we can start promoting the event that will be…" Viola trailed off, her expression questioning.

"The tree lighting is on Saturday the fourteenth, so we'll have the first Cocoa Crawl and Dickens Holiday of Lights on Sunday to keep the momentum going," Elise answered. "The second one will be on Saturday the twenty-first, drawing shoppers to do their last-minute shopping."

Enthusiasm appeared to be high, and Giles gave Elise a thumbs-up.

"Let's end this meeting so that we can enjoy our wonderful desserts," Karla suggested.

Elise was tempted to throw her arms around Giles's neck and kiss him. She walked back to Sebastian, Axel, and Giles. "I feel like I've been through a war without ammunition."

"Me, too. I'm determined to make that woman eat her words," Axel declared. "Giles, where did you come up with that Cocoa Crawl idea?"

"A friend of mine ran a similar event for a couple of his restaurants, but the hot chocolate had a little more kick than whipped cream and marshmallows. In the end, they had to throw darts at balloons to win a prize. I toned it down to a small-town idea."

"Not that the other event doesn't sound like fun," Axel chuckled. "Your idea pacified those hard-nosed women. I'm going to pass on the coffee, using the excuse to check on the kids. Sebastian, if you're smart, you'll get out of Dodge with me."

"Before you go downstairs, there's a tray of goodies and drinks in the kitchen for the kiddies," Elise told them.

After they walked away, she took advantage of a few moments alone with Giles. "It would be very inappropriate if I threw my arms around your neck and gave you a big kiss."

"I'll take a rain check on your idea." He wiggled his eyebrows.

"I've lost sleep worrying about this meeting, knowing who and what I was facing. You are Viola's favorite person in the whole world."

"I'd rather be your favorite person in the whole world."

A blush warmed her cheeks. "What a nice thing to say. I'll write up all the particulars they need to start publicizing tomorrow. I'll also put it on our website and social media. Now, I could use some coffee and, if there are any left, a couple of your mini crepes."

A little before nine o'clock, they got into Giles's SUV. A dusting of snow had fallen, but the wintry moon reappeared, brightening the night sky. Giles kept to just below the speed limit, and she decided he was a good driver.

"Did everyone have a good time this evening?" Elise asked the kids.

"I put some ideas together for the event center logo," Emile said, "but I'm not ready to share them yet. They need a little more tweaking."

"By any chance, have you worked on my candy character?" Giles asked the teenager.

"Yeah, but that really needs a lot of tweaking."

"Mr. Giles, I'm going to be playing soccer after school this Thursday," Sophie said. "This is our last game for the season. Could you come and watch me?"

"I'd love to see you play. Tell me where and what time."

"I'll be going, too, so you can ride with me," Elise invited.

He'd done it again, being kind and considerate. What he'd done to placate the troublemakers and get them to accept the Dickens light show had truly been amazing. Whatever his previous job had been, he had the skills of a mediator.

He pulled into their driveway and kept the headlights on so they could see as they went into the dark house.

"Mommy, our house looks so sad without the decorations. Mr. Giles, your house looks sad, too."

"I was thinking the same thing," Emile added.

"I agree. If you had a choice, how would you decorate your house?" Giles asked the kids.

"I'd like some of those cool lights that flash to the beat of music," Emile said.

"I want snowmen and a big Santa and candy canes!"

"Give them an inch, and they take a mile," Elise said with a laugh. "There are quite a few light displays that weren't used for our light show. Maybe we can use some of them. Both of you go into the house and take your showers. Emile first. I'll be right in. I want to talk to Mr. Giles."

"Night, Mr. Giles!" the kids called out together.

Elise turned to Giles. "Thank you again for what you did this evening. Did you act as a mediator in your previous job?"

"You mean like a contract negotiator? No. It just comes naturally."

"It's a wonderful gift. If you're not busy tomorrow, would you go with me to the event center to select lights for the front of our houses?"

"I'd like that, but only if we can set up the lights before the kids come home from school. It will be a great surprise."

"Deal. We'll leave around nine o'clock, but take both cars." She reached for the handle but then turned back to him. Was she being too bold…? Too late. "Any chance you want to cash in on that rain check?"

"I'd love that." He grinned and leaned close to share a good-night kiss. His warm hand settled on her cheek, keeping their lips together longer than she'd intended.

"Giles DeLuc," she said with a sigh, removing her arms from around his neck, "making crepes isn't the only thing you're good at. Night."

Chapter 8

Giles followed Elise down a narrow paved road leading to the rear of the depot, which ended in front of two new metal storage buildings. The temperature had dropped drastically overnight, and it was currently fifteen degrees. His introduction to putting up Christmas lights outside meant freezing his butt off. It didn't matter. He was doing this for the kids.

A black pickup truck was parked close to the building. He met Elise when she got out of her car. She'd bundled up for the day. Their booted feet crunched in the snow as they headed toward the door next to a wide garage door opening.

"That's Shawn's truck. He had to be here today and said he'd help us load the boxes into our vehicles."

She pulled open the metal door, and they stepped into the large space. Jets of warm air coming from a heater suspended from the ceiling chased the chill from their bodies. Just off to the right was an office/workshop.

The sound and lighting engineer was sitting at his desk, working on a laptop. A zippered quilted vest covered his gray, wine-plaid flannel shirt. His black watch cap covered his salt-and-pepper hair, which brushed the curves of his ears.

"Good morning, Elise, Giles," he greeted and lowered the black-framed glasses that he'd pushed to his forehead. "I was happy to get your email confirming we're a go for the light show. Putting out the lights before the ground froze was a smart move. I was out here last night, double-checking the timers, and everything is working like clockwork. The kids are going to squeal their heads off when they see those lights."

Four words plowed over Giles's enthusiasm—"*before the ground froze*." He told himself not to panic.

Elise gave Giles an appreciative smile before turning back to Shawn. "It was an uphill battle, but our friend here sweet-talked the troublemakers into accepting the Dickens Holiday of Lights."

"As you know, Axel and Sebastian went a little overboard ordering displays. I went through the extras and set aside what you might want to use. They're all in boxes, and each one comes with its own solar-powered unit."

"Shawn, before going any further, any suggestions on how we're supposed to handle the frozen-ground problem?" Giles asked.

"Have you ever used an auger to drill holes in the ice when you went ice fishing?" he asked Giles.

"I've never used an auger or gone ice fishing." Once again, he was in over his head. He needed to get out of the kitchen more often.

Shawn turned his laptop around and brought up a picture of an electric auger. “This battery-powered baby can drill holes in the ground for the stakes that hold up the figurines. I have extra batteries that hold the charge a lot longer.”

“I think I can handle that.” *I hope.*

“I can’t let you have all the fun,” Elise teased Giles. “Let’s have a look at what you selected,” she said to Shawn.

Shawn had spread out the boxes along the back wall. “We have nutcrackers, reindeer, gingerbread men, a family of snow people, Santa riding his sleigh. The huge candy canes and white Christmas trees look spectacular when lighted.” He moved to the end of the row. “This wasn’t ordered, but we were charged, so Axel said to hold on to it. It’s a set of five large lawn signs with an old-fashioned steam engine and four train cars. The engineer is a gingerbread man. They’re all connected by huge, colorful, gumdrop-shaped lights. A big space is needed to get the best effect of the layout.”

Giles loved the sign setup but wanted to wait for Elise to select what she’d like to use to decorate the front of her house. “Elise, you get first dibs.”

She walked slowly back and forth, studying the pictures on the boxes. “I love the tall candy canes and trees. Sophie would want the snow family, Santa and his sleigh, with the reindeer.”

“I have an idea,” Shawn said. “Create an arch with the candy canes. Santa’s sleigh and the reindeer can ride through it. Surround the snow family figurines with the white Christmas trees."

"I love that idea," Elise said.

"I'll go with the lawn signs and a few of the gingerbread men," Giles already pictured the setup in his head.

"Your houses will look great," Shawn said. "I'll put together a sketch to make it easier when you're placing them on the lawn. Also, once you get the small solar panel staked, it's going to take a few hours to fully charge. Hopefully, the sun will stay out the rest of the day."

"I hadn't thought of that," Elise admitted.

Shawn hesitated. "I know you two are eager to use that power auger, but I'm free for the rest of the day. Do you want some help?"

Giles raised a brow at Elise. "We'd be stupid if we didn't accept help. Remember, we'd like to surprise the children when they get home from school."

"Shawn, your help would be much appreciated, but you won't work for free and don't argue with us," Elise said.

An hour later, they started putting up the lights in front of Elise's house. Thankfully, there were only three inches of undisturbed snow on the ground.

Giles didn't know what to expect when he attempted to drill his first hole, but he put two glove-covered hands on the handle of the auger and held on tight. He'd like to say it was smooth as butter, but he felt the resistance when the bit hit the frozen ground, and the drill ate away at the frozen surface.

He enjoyed a sense of accomplishment. “One down, a couple hundred to go.” The blue sky wasn’t threatened by clouds, but he briefly eyed the sun. “Pour out some extra power.”

The drilling and placement went smoothly. They laid out the pieces following Shawn’s drawing. With experience, the tech connected each solar-powered unit as soon as it was stable in the ground. The frozen snow also helped to support the bases.

Working together, they finished the front of Elise’s house by noon.

Giles shoved his hands in his pockets and stood closer to the road to get a better look at the display. “This looks amazing. Creating a faux arch with candy canes was a great idea.” He looked at Elise. The cold had made her cheeks red.

“Sophie is going to jump out of her skin,” she noted with a very big smile.

“There will be fewer holes to drill for Giles’s displays, so it won’t take long to set them up,” Shawn told them.

Elise checked her watch. “It’s a little after noon. It’s time to stop and have lunch. How about grilled cheese sandwiches and homemade tomato soup to warm up our chilled bodies?”

“Sounds great,” Giles agreed.

While eating, they found out a little more about the lighting and sound engineer.

Shawn was fifty-five years old and had been married to an actress for fifteen years. She'd focused on her career and never wanted to have a family. During the two years the theaters were closed because of the pandemic, she had wanted to keep in shape and had started running each morning in Central Park. She was killed by a mugger. The person who did it had not been found. His Aunt Matilda had encouraged him to move to Dickens, and he'd never been happier.

When they walked outside, Elise picked up the auger. "My turn! You had all the fun earlier."

Shawn put his hands on his hips and laughed. "You two really like my power tool. Ask Santa for one."

Once again, they laid out the pieces, making sure there was enough space for the lighted gumdrops.

"Giles, are you aware that this display has an extra Bluetooth power pack? You can download the app on your phone, and the lights will pulse to any music. You can also set a timer like the ones we have at the depot."

Giles gave a thumbs up. "Looks like we'll be able to fulfill Emile's request."

"That means we'll be making both my kids happy." Elise gripped the handle of the auger. "Gentlemen, let's get this done! The school bus gets here at three thirty."

Setting up the display in front of Giles's house went faster. He was grateful that Shawn was so skilled at connecting the wiring with the added features. He was more than pleased with how the display turned out, especially with the gingerbread men spaced sporadically about the area. It also gave him a new idea—using fresh ginger to flavor a dessert crepe.

Once again, they stood back to admire the display. Elise looped her arm around Giles's elbow. "I don't know which one I like better."

"They both look great." Giles checked his watch. "Nothing like cutting it close. The bus will be here in fifteen minutes."

"I hate to rain on our parade, but like I mentioned this morning, these units won't be powered up enough for any light show this evening," Shawn reminded them.

"My children will be happy when they see these decorations. Shawn, we can't thank you enough for helping today."

"It's my pleasure. I never had this kind of fun when I lived in the city. I get to help my aunt set up the trees at her shop, too."

Giles tapped his bottom lip. "How are you at making snowmen?"

"I haven't made one since I was a kid. Why?"

"I've entered the snowman-making contest after the tree lighting ceremony. Elise, Sophie, and Emile are helping me. We could use an extra pair of hands."

"I'd be delighted!"

The sound of the school bus coming down the road drew their attention. Giles hadn't experienced the excitement of a child very much, but he was feeling it now. His feet were frozen, and his fingertips were numb. The door opened, and Sophie's squeal and smile made it all worth it.

She ran up the front walk leading to her house and dropped her backpack on the ground. "Mommy! Mr. Giles! Just what I wanted! Candy canes! Santa!" She threw her arms around Elise's waist. "These are the bestest Christmas displays ever!"

"We're so glad you like them. Mr. Murphy helped us."

"Thanks, Mr. Murphy." She gave him a quick hug, too.

"You're welcome," the tech replied, returning her hug.

"Sophie, the lights are solar-powered," Giles said. "They get their energy from the sun, so they might not light up tonight."

"That's okay, Mr. Giles. I love them."

"Mama, take my picture standing under the candy canes so I can show it to my friends. Then I want to stand next to the train engine and the gingerbread men!"

Giles was much relieved when the impromptu photo session ended. The wind had picked up, and the temperature had definitely dropped.

"Can I interest everyone in a cup of hot chocolate?" Elise asked.

"Thanks, Elise," Shawn said, "but I have to head over to Aunt Matilda's shop. I check stock every afternoon and replenish the shelves. See you Monday night at the open house."

"I'm going to beg off, too," Giles said. "I have a number of emails to confirm deliveries from my distributors and pay bills. I'll also download the app for the Christmas lights and will make sure I get music the kids like. Sophie, what's your favorite Christmas song?"

"'Rockin' Around the Christmas Tree.' My brother likes 'You're a Mean One, Mr. Grinch.' He always plays it because Jamie's father was the Grinch."

"Elise, what's your favorite song?" Giles asked.

"The Nat King Cole version of 'The Christmas Song.'"

"I'll make sure those songs are at the top of the playlist."

Giles watched them walk into the house. Things were falling into place better than he had ever imagined. Now, he had to figure out how to get his former sister-in-law to back off.

Like a little child waiting for Santa, he kept peeking out the front window, hoping the energy packs had charged enough for the lights to come on. While eating dinner, he watched the weather report. The weatherman wasn't their friend. A snowstorm was heading their way, with the possibility of six to eight inches of snow over the weekend.

He texted Shawn, worried about how that would affect the solar panels. The tech called and said there wouldn't be a problem. The solar panels could generate electricity even when covered with snow. Sunlight would still reach the panels, keeping the solar cells producing energy.

The solar-powered units were fully charged by Thursday. When they got home from the soccer game, the display washed away Sophie's disappointment that her team hadn't won. Her smile got even bigger when the gumdrop lights flashed to the beat of "Rockin' Around the Christmas Tree."

Elise invited Giles to dinner afterward. He'd never had a more delicious chicken pot pie.

He'd been seriously considering the selections on his crepe menu. Having tasted and enjoyed the unique flavors of dinner crepes while visiting France, he realized he was leaning too heavily toward "fancy" selections. Elise had prepared pot pie and a delicious beef stew. He was also living in New England, where people enjoyed comfort foods in the winter. His dinner menu currently offers eight selections, and two would suit the area better.

Saturday morning at ten, Giles parked his SUV in the Gridley's Farm parking area. Based on the number of cars, the place was packed. He didn't know who was more excited, the kids or him.

Mother Nature had sent the temperature to the high twenties, and the sun was bright. Luckily, the predicted six to eight inches of snow had been only two. Trudging through the snow to pick out a tree would be less uncomfortable.

Elise released her seat belt and turned to look at the children in the back seat. "Both of you, wear your gloves and hats, and no arguing. Don't wander off!"

"I want to go to the petting zoo!" Sophie announced. "Holly and Ivy said to make sure I wear my boots because there's animal poop on the ground."

"Sophie, we'll get to that. I went on their website. The petting zoo is very popular. They only let in so many kids at once. Tickets are stamped with the time you can enter the petting area."

"Let's get our tree first, then we can take our time doing the fun activities," Giles suggested. "I went on their website, too, and you can roast marshmallows at special fire pits. It will be my treat."

"I agree with Mr. Giles. Remember what we talked about. We don't have room for a Griswold-size Christmas tree!"

"Really? I was hoping mine would come complete with a squirrel," Giles teased.

"You're all right, Mr. Giles," Emile said, giving him a high five.

They approached the wood-framed building to the right of the petting zoo, which housed the gift shop. Smoke from the fire pits spiced the air.

"Welcome to Gridley's!"

"Hi, Tom," Elise said with a big smile. "You know, Giles."

The owner's black and red wool hat bore the tree farm's logo. The colors in his hat matched his black and red plaid wool coat. Giles removed his glove and held out a hand.

"Quite a place you've got here. This is a first for both of us, getting a live tree."

"We make it as accommodating as possible." Tom pointed to a horse-drawn wagon that had just pulled to the side of the building. People were getting off, and a line had formed for the next riders. "Hop on a wagon, and you'll be taken out to the fields. Once you select a tree, holler, 'Here,' and one of the Paul Bunyan on our staff will tag the tree, cut it down, and bring it to the parking area."

"Can we cut it down ourselves?" Emile asked.

"Sure," Tom let the teenager know.

"Before we start our grand tree adventure," Elise said to Tom, "I want to let you know that our plan to establish the Dickens Historical Evergreen Preserve is a go. As we discussed, we'll celebrate Arbor Day with the first tree planting."

"I love the idea, Elise," Tom said. "I'm sorry I couldn't attend the Historical Society meeting, but I heard, via the gossip, that your plan is a go. We can discuss the details closer to April."

"Tom, since you're the tree expert, do you have any suggestions on what type of Christmas tree we should select?" Giles asked.

"The Fraser fir will last about five weeks, and the Douglas fir will still look good for four weeks. Your choice. All of the trees are beautiful. The wagon driver stops and announces the name of the individual fields."

"Thanks again." Giles noticed another wagon had just pulled in, and the line to get on wasn't long. "Come on. Let's get on this wagon."

The families sitting on bales of hay that lined the flat trailer shared the excitement of selecting a tree. They bounced over the ruts and snow "rocks" on the dirt road. He didn't mind that Elise swayed and pressed her cheek against his shoulder.

"Sorry."

"Not a problem. We can share body warmth with us packed in like sardines in a can."

"There is that," she agreed. "Have you decided on what kind of tree you want?"

"No. You select yours first, and I'll get a different one. We'll see which one stays fresh the longest."

"That's a good idea." Elise frowned. "Are you always so accommodating and thoughtful? You let me select the Christmas lights first. At the last minute, Emile decided he wanted to attend the soccer game at his sister's school, so you volunteered to pick him up from the bus. You make sure your holiday lights play the songs we like, and now you want me to select the tree I want first. I'm only getting started. Are you trying to kill me with kindness?"

Elise clamped a gloved hand over her mouth. "Oh, Giles, I'm so sorry. That was a terrible thing for me to say. I'm just not used to…"

What she'd claimed gave him pause. Was he going overboard with being thoughtful and accommodating, hoping she would like him? None of what he'd done had been forced or phony. She and her kids had brought so much happiness into his life.

Though, he was only kidding himself. The bottom line was that she'd hate him when she learned why he'd come to Dickens. For now, he'd selfishly savor the happiness he enjoyed when being with them and doing things together.

He squeezed her gloved hand. "I'm just being me. I'll back off if you feel I've gotten too close to you and the children too quickly."

"No, absolutely not. My children have grown quite fond of you…and I have, too."

"I'm very happy to hear that, but if you're ever uncomfortable with something I've said or done, tell me, and I'll back off. Now, what type of tree do you want?"

"Fraser fir, and our tree will last longer than yours!"

Walking between the rows of trees wasn't as difficult as Elise had anticipated. Much of the snow had been tamped down by earlier tree hunters. Some of Elise's enthusiasm had dampened as she thought about what she'd said earlier to Giles. Speaking her mind so openly had come out before she'd given much thought to what she'd said. She'd practically called him out for being kind and thoughtful! Then he'd apologized!

She closed her mind to what had happened when she heard Sophie yell, "Mommy, I found our tree."

Emile called out at the same time.

She glanced between the two trees, which were both perfect. In the end, she had to do eeny, meeny, miny, mo.

Then they all hollered, "Here!"

"I'm cutting it down," Emile reminded them.

The cutter arrived with the handsaw but stood back to let Emile do the honors. She took pictures of Emile getting down on his hands and knees to saw at the trunk. The cutter put a tag on the tree and would have it delivered to the area next to the parking lot. They got back on the wagon and rode to a different area so Giles could select his tree. They followed the same procedure and called for a cutter.

Standing next to a magnificent Douglas fir, Giles put a hand to his back. “I hurt my back the other day when we were setting up the lights.” He winked at Elise. “Emile, any chance you can give me a hand cutting down this tree? I’ll hold the top while you man the saw.”

“Sure, Mr. Giles.”

He hadn’t hurt his back the other day, and she knew what he was doing. *Thoughtful and considerate.*

They took the wagon back to the welcome center, where they got their petting zoo tickets and bags of special feed for the animals. Giles purchased four s’mores-making kits.

“Are you going to join us?” she asked Giles, passing Sophie and Emile small cloth bags of feed.

“Why not?” As they headed toward the fenced-in animal paddock, he asked Sophie, “Do you have a favorite animal? They have sheep, goats, ducks and geese.”

“I want to pet them all!” the nine-year-old announced and ran ahead.

Wire mesh on the inside of the post-and-rail fence protected the animals from curious visitors. A chorus of duck and goose squawks announced that the critters were happy with the attention they were getting.

“Thank you for joining us today,” Elise said to Giles while she leaned against the paddock where the baby goats were housed, keeping an eye on her daughter and son.

"It's been a lot of fun."

"Sharing this time with you has made our day extra special." Her gloved fingers interlaced with his and squeezed. "I saw right through your ruse, pretending you hurt your back."

She definitely embarrassed him.

"Mom, check the time on our tickets," Emile called out.

"It's our turn. Let's pet some animals—beware of animal droppings."

She enjoyed interacting with and feeding the animals as much as her kids did. Giles, too, couldn't stop smiling. She determined that the baby goats were his favorite.

"Mommy, I'd like to have a goat for a pet," Sophie said as they left the fenced-in area.

"You have a cat, and I think Simone would be jealous." She quickly followed up with, "We're going to make s'mores at the fire pits. First, we have to go to the bathroom and wash our hands."

"Don't be insulted, but it will probably take you two longer to get cleaned up than Emile and me. I'll take the bag, and we'll be at one of the fire pits."

"No insult taken."

Giles claimed a fire pit that could accommodate a family of six. A short wall of cinderblocks encompassed the fire, and large boulders provided seating. A barrel of water and a fire extinguisher were close by.

Emile added two pieces of wood to the fire. "This is perfect. The last time I made s'mores was when I was twelve years old. My aunt and uncle built a fire pit in the backyard."

"I've never actually made one, but I have seen them made on television."

Sophie pointed to a ring of rocks. "Mr. Giles, that's the keep-back fire zone. I'm a Girl Scout. We had to earn our fire-building badge."

"Thank you for giving me instructions."

Elise picked up a long metal skewer and slowly slid a puffy marshmallow onto the pointed end. "Now I'll demonstrate how to make the perfect s'more." She slowly turned the spongy confection over the flames, which gave off just enough heat to roast but not burn the sweet treat. The outer skin had turned a golden brown when she ordered, "Giles, grab the graham crackers and chocolate!"

He quickly moved in, and she sandwiched her perfection between the two crackers.

"For you, Mr. Kind and Considerate." She grinned, holding it out to him.

"Thank you, but ladies first," he said, passing it to Sophie. Then he winked at Emile. "We watched an expert. Let's make our own."

Elise stood to the side and gave him a silent pat on the back. He'd actually paid attention to her demonstration. "So, how do you like your s'more?" she asked him after he'd gotten his first taste.

"Gooey, sweet confection." Melted chocolate escaped the corner of Giles's mouth, but he caught it with his tongue. "One is enough."

After wiping away the evidence of chocolate and marshmallow from Sophie's face and hands, they headed home with two trees securely tied to the top of Giles's SUV. Their jackets had absorbed the woodsy scent from the fire. They'd just brought the trees into the houses when it started to snow.

Elise decided it was the perfect way to end the perfect day.

Chapter 9

Giles walked into his house, tired but satisfied. Tomorrow was his open house. Fifty invitations had gone out, and forty-five people had responded. Everyone was looking forward to tasting his wonderful crepes.

It felt good working in the kitchen, getting back to his roots. He'd spent all day preparing the fillings. Because of the volume needed, he'd also prepped the batters and another recipe for his special chocolate and salted caramel dessert crepe. The commercial freezer was fully stocked with French vanilla and chocolate ice cream.

He was worried. The pastry chef he'd hired was supposed to have shown up this morning to help prep for tomorrow, but he'd been a no-show. There was no way Giles could handle the open house alone.

He left four messages with the guy but hadn't gotten a response. He'd Zoomed the initial interview. The guy had said he planned to relocate to Portland, Maine and had no problem with the hour-long commute. His references had given glowing reports about him.

Giles had also sent reminder messages to the two waitresses, making sure they would arrive at three p.m. so he could review what was expected of them during the open house. He'd provide white shirts, black trousers, and red string ties. His plan was to prepare some of the meals and circulate among the guests. His main focus would be to gather feedback on how much they liked or didn't like what they'd eaten.

If he said he wasn't nervous, he'd be lying. He'd opened five-star luxury restaurants around the country—Chicago, New York, LA, San Francisco, Dallas—and had never been this nervous. Then again, he'd had assistants who'd helped make the grand openings successful.

Creperie de Dickens was the most important. This was his alone. Success or failure rested on his shoulders. People could show up tomorrow night and not like what he'd prepared.

He'd always remember one of the most important things his grandmother had told him: *You shouldn't expect to please everyone with your cooking. People have different expectations and tastes. Critics can make or break an establishment. If someone tells you they don't like something, you shouldn't take immediate offense. You should turn the tables and ask what they don't like about the dish. You might be able to squash a negative comment before it happens. People are honored if you take the time to ask them.*

He fixed a cup of coffee and carried it into the living room. Except for a couple of armchairs, an end table, and a lamp, the only thing that stood out was his beautiful Douglas fir in the center of the front window. The pleasant scent from the fresh tree lingered throughout the house.

Yesterday, they decorated Elise's tree first, and then they came over to his house. The kids had been excited and insisted they share some of the ornaments they hadn't used. He'd never gotten back to Trim-A-Tree to get additional ornaments. He thought the tree was so beautifully shaped that only white lights were needed. They'd then invited him back to their house to have pizza Elise had made. The day and the evening had been perfect.

He sat in the armchair and stretched out his legs. He was tired but not ready to go to bed. He booted up the laptop that he'd left on the end table. This would be a good time for him to do some research on Elise's house. In his mind, the previous owner should have been aware of the home's historical value as an added selling point and shared it with the realtor.

He typed in Ringing Rocks House, but the first search result was Ringing Rocks Park in Upper Black Eddy, Pennsylvania.

Next, he entered Elise's address into the archive of the County Historical Society. According to the records, there was a "stone house that made noise." It had been a hotel frequented by passengers traveling from Canada to Boston. This made sense since the railroad depot was only a couple of miles down the road. Another note mentioned the house had been a brothel for a brief time. The sheriff had raided the establishment and shut it down for a few months. It had reopened as Dickens Lodging.

He wasn't about to tell Elise her house had once been a place of ill repute.

He scrolled a little more and found a grainy black-and-white photo with a printed notation that said, "Dickens Lodging—the stone house that was reported to make noise." The house definitely resembled her home.

Another very old photo was of a hotel registry. The fancy script had faded, making the handwriting difficult to decipher. He tapped on the screen to enlarge the photo as much as possible, trying to read the names. His finger paused, and he squinted a little. The name he was trying to decipher was C. Dickens.

He jerked back in the chair. No way, but that would mean Charles Dickens had arrived at the depot! Maybe his eyes were just tired. The script wasn't the best. Maybe it was only wishful thinking on his part. He studied the name again, and it was still not clearly decipherable. He wouldn't share this information with Elise right away. He would wait until he had more proof. He'd like nothing better than to have the old biddies eat their words.

He wanted to keep researching but yawned a couple of times and decided to call it a night. He copied and pasted everything into a document, including the page link. Before shutting down, he clicked the link to join the society. He chuckled. Now, he belonged to two historical societies.

He turned off the tree lights and looked out the window. The lawn lights would be going off at eleven o'clock.

Monday afternoon, Giles listened for a second time to the message from the man he'd hired to be his pastry chef. "I've decided to take a different job in Chicago. I got an unexpected call from Bascom, the restaurant conglomerate. I applied to them months ago but haven't heard back. They contacted me yesterday and are desperate for a pastry chef at the flagship restaurant. They've doubled what you were going to pay me, and they're covering my relocation costs."

Giles tossed his cell phone onto the polished wood surface of his workstation. This couldn't be happening. He was positive his backstabbing former sister-in-law had had something to do with him losing his pastry chef.

As of right now, he was without a pastry chef or servers. The two sisters had called earlier to let him know they had the flu.

He turned at the quick knock at the back door, just off his small kitchen. He hadn't bothered to lock it, so he called out, "Come in."

"Hi, are you ready for tonight?" Elise carried a cardboard holder with two hot cups. "I brought you hot chocolate." When he didn't return her smile, she asked, "What's wrong?"

"As of right now, I don't have an assistant pastry chef or servers. The one I hired took a job in Chicago, and my servers have the flu."

"Oh, Giles, how terrible!" She stepped close and casually wrapped her arm around his waist. "What happened to the pastry chef you hired?"

"Out of the blue, he got a call from Bascom, a Chicago-based restaurant conglomerate. They doubled what I offered to pay him."

"Even I've heard of Bascom. They can squash a restaurant's reputation with their big toe!"

Now I know what being squashed by a big toe feels like. He stepped away and threw his arms wide. "No way can I do everything myself," he said, not bothering to hide his frustration. "I have five dinner selections, one brunch, and two dessert crepes. I prepared the fillings yesterday. Don't suggest I make the crepes and heat them up before serving them! The objective is to make them fresh."

"First of all, I'd never suggest you make them ahead of time." Elise jammed her hands on her hips. "My grandmother would be shooting darts down from heaven." She paused to study the workstation he'd set up with six crepe makers. In the rear were bins that would hold the sauces and fillings. "Very neat setup. Each unit has its own leveling wand. I take it two of the six will be specifically for the dessert crepes?"

"Yes. I don't want to take the chance any of the fillings might distort the flavor, even though I wipe down the surface after each use."

"We followed the same procedure in my grandmother's commercial kitchen. How about I give you a hand this evening?"

He'd never even considered asking Elise, but he was desperate. "Are you sure? I'll pay you for the evening."

"Giles DeLuc! Now you're being insulting! My crepes might not be as perfect as yours, but I can handle the batter you prepared."

"Sorry. I didn't mean to insult you. I'm sure your crepes will be perfect. What about the kids?"

"I'll ask Karla if they can stay with her. This event is over at eight o'clock. Let me call her now."

Inside, his temper was churning. How had his sister-in-law found out about his plans to open a creperie? He'd maintained his friendships with the people he'd worked with at Bascom, so he'd be making a couple of phone calls. He'd also have to start advertising for another pastry chef.

"Thanks, Karla." Elise ended the call. "She said not a problem. The baby is cranky from teething, so she doesn't want to bring him this evening. The only stipulation is you make her one of everything so she can sample the crepes."

"Great! Now all I have to do is find two servers."

"I know where you can find two."

"Sebastian and Axel?" he blurted.

"No, Lars and Jens. I heard them say the other night that they'd be glad to help you out. We can give them a crash course on handing out the menu and serving the food."

"I just thought of something. Do you think Emile would like to make a few bucks this evening? He can be a busboy and clean off the tables."

"I'm sure he'd be delighted. He wants to get his girlfriend a special Christmas gift, so that will be an extra incentive."

"Let me check with the guys." He was still nervous about this evening, but thanks to Elise, some of his stress had subsided. "First, I could really use a hug and one of your misdirected kisses."

She stepped close and slipped her arms around him. "We both could use a hug, and I'd love to share one of my misdirected kisses."

He lowered his head and brought their mouths together in a slow, easy kiss. Elise pressed her lips a little harder against his mouth. It took everything in him not to moan his delight at her eagerness to return his affection. He reluctantly ended the kiss.

"Thank you for doing this. I couldn't have handled it alone."

"That's what friends are for. Now, why don't you call Lars and Jens? I have to go home and meet the school bus. I'll take Sophie to Karla's and bring Emile back with me."

At 4:50, he closed the last button on his chef's jacket and walked out to the dining room. The tree lights showed through the open vertical blinds, and the votive candles glowed softly in the red glass holders.

Emile finished placing the last bottles of spring water on the tables. He wore a white shirt, black trousers, and a red string tie.

"Thanks for helping out at the last minute," Giles said.

"I've never done anything like this. Do you want me to hand out the menus when people sit down? I can say, 'Welcome to Creperie de Dickens.'"

"That would be great. For this evening, it's only a single sheet."

The teenager reached into his back pocket and pulled out a piece of paper. "I made a logo for you last evening."

"My licorice character?"

"I'm still working on that. This is for your shop. If you don't like it, that's okay. I can change it. I showed it to my mom, and she said it's perfect."

Giles was overwhelmed.

Emile had centered the letter D on the flat surface of a crepe pan. A spatula and wooden spoon crisscrossed under the letter. Arched above the logo were the words *Creperie de Dickens*.

"Emile, this is awesome. I'll put it at the top of my menus when they're printed."

The teenager blushed slightly. “Thanks, Mr. Giles, for believing in me.”

At exactly five p.m., Elise walked out of the kitchen, wearing a white chef’s jacket. “Normally, when a performer is going onstage, they’re told to break a leg. In this case, knock ’em dead, crepe man.”

“Emile, open the door for our guests.”

The stream of invited guests was slow but steady. He could tell they enjoyed what they’d eaten. Emile brought back empty plates.

“You’ve only got another half hour,” Elise told Giles. “Why don’t you put on your clean chef jacket and mingle with your guests? I’ve got this. If I need help, Emile will let you know.”

“Thanks, Elise.”

He walked into the small bathroom, washed his hands, and combed his hair before putting on a clean jacket. So far, the feedback about the food had been positive. From his count, thirty guests had been served, and the other ten were currently seated. He’d spent a little time earlier mingling with his guests and had been quite impressed by Lars’s and Jens’s interactions with the people enjoying the food.

When they arrived a little after three o'clock, he gave them a crash course on the various crepes and fillings that would be available in case they had any questions. After serving the food, they would go back a few minutes later to ask if the patrons were enjoying their meal.

The newspaper editor said she'd contact him for a one-on-one interview. Axel, Freja, Sebastian, and Jamie each gave him a double thumbs-up. The mayor and her husband said Giles's unique restaurant would add a special flavor to dining options in their fair town. Shawn joined his aunt, Matilda Cudworth, and Amy Doritt. They loved the dinner options but favored the dessert crepes with ice cream.

Giles stepped into the dining room and saw Emile carrying a tray of dirty dishes. He was proud of the teenager.

"Emile, you're doing a great job."

"Mr. Giles, people are leaving money on the table, so I've put it in a jar in the kitchen."

"That money is yours. Jens and Lars are aware of the tips and want you to have the money."

The teenager's eyes widened. "But there's a bunch of money in the jar!"

"The guys told me they're having fun, enjoying this change of pace since they don't normally have a chance to mingle with customers. Many of the same people enjoy their pastries. If you have any money left over from buying a gift for Hailey, buy something for your mother and sister."

"Thanks, Mr. Giles. That's a great idea. Three ladies are sitting at a table and asked if I could give you a message. They want to talk to you."

"I know who they are," he replied with a heavy sigh.

He pasted on a smile and approached their table. "Ladies, how are you enjoying the food?"

"Giles, I have to be totally honest. I never knew so much could be done with a crepe," Sadie Prince said with a beaming smile.

He noticed Lars had just served their dessert crepes, his signature salted caramel with vanilla ice cream.

"Do you see any catering in your future?" Viola asked. "I'd love to plan a dinner party with you, making the crepes right in front of my guests."

"Will we have to make reservations if we want to come to the creperie for dinner?" Tillie Doyle asked.

"I don't plan to do any catering, and reservations won't be necessary at the present time." *I won't even be opening next week if I don't find a pastry chef.* "If you'll excuse me, I should speak to my other guests. Thank you for coming."

After the last few guests left, he locked the front door and returned to the kitchen. Emile set a tray by the commercial dishwasher. Lars and Jens put empty bottles of spring water in the recycling bin. They'd gone through almost all of the fillings he'd prepared, and Elise was wiping off the crepe machines. He couldn't have asked for a more efficient team of helpers.

"I can't thank you all enough for helping out," Giles said. "Can I make you something to eat?"

"We had a lot of fun, and Elise made us crepes earlier," Lars answered. "Giles, you have something great here. Your guests raved about the crepes and are eager to return as regulars."

"We're so glad you decided to move to Dickens," Jens added.

"Me, too. Now I have to try to find a pastry chef by next week for my grand opening."

"We can make a few calls," Lars offered. "We've got to get going. Have to get our beauty sleep."

Jens handed Emile the dollar bills that had been left on one of the tables. "Add this to your stash."

He clutched the dollar bills in his hand. "Mom, all the tip money is mine!"

"You worked hard, and I'm so proud of you."

"Mr. Giles loved the logo I made for him and will have it printed on his menus."

"I was pretty sure he'd like it. Are you hungry?"

"I'd like one of those breakfast crepes with sausage, egg, and fancy potatoes. I'll also take a chocolate one with chocolate ice cream."

Giles took Elise by the hand and brought her over to one of the chairs by the small table he'd arranged in the corner of the room.

"Sit! I'll make Emile's crepes. You've worked hard this evening. While he's eating, I'll finish cleaning up."

"It'd been a while since I'd made that many crepes," she admitted, "but it all came back. I had a lot of fun, too."

"I don't know how I can repay you."

She held up a hand, palm out. "Don't start. No payment is necessary."

In no time at all, he prepared the teenager's request. "Mr. Giles, these breakfast ones are as good as the ones my mom makes."

"Emile, yours is the best and most important of all the compliments I received this evening."

A half-hour later, Giles was alone in his shop. For a day that had started out badly, it had turned into a great evening. He'd started the commercial dishwasher with the last load of plates and bowls. His second, smaller dishwasher was for glasses only.

A few of his guests had asked if there would be other drink options. He planned on offering a couple of herbal teas and specialty ciders in the future.

He turned off the lights in his clean kitchen, picked up his glass of ice water, and sat at one of the tables. He'd closed the vertical blinds and enjoyed looking at the tree lights that he'd yet to turn off.

His friends had all come together, making his open house a success. When he'd opened his other restaurants, he'd been eager to read the reviews, anticipating any negativity. But not tonight. His best compliment had come from a fourteen-year-old boy. Lingering guilt still lay heavy on his shoulders because he hadn't confessed to Elise why he'd really come to Dickens.

He checked his watch, noting the time in Chicago was an hour earlier. Someone was out to destroy his plans to start anew. He reached for his cell phone and made the first call.

"Bascom." Elise had muttered the name too many times since Giles had said the name the evening of his open house. They were going to the tree lighting together and planned to meet him at his house in a few minutes.

"Bascom. They almost destroyed Giles's opening of his little shop, too."

They'd flicked her and Claude away like pesky flies, destroying their chances to purchase the property for their little restaurant. The realtor had let them know that another buyer was interested in the building. Claude had found out the competitor's identity and knew their dreams could never be achieved.

Then he was killed, and the rest of her nightmare continued, the demands for repaying his extravagant loan. She'd left town before the restaurant conglomerate had started the renovations on the building. She couldn't think of what might have been.

Tonight was the tree lighting, followed by the snowman-making contest. Tomorrow would also be the first day of the Cocoa Crawl. She'd volunteered to help 2 Sisters Kringle and Fudge with the expected influx of holiday customers. Sophie and Lynnie would be there to help, too. Axel had asked Emile and Hailey if they could help Holly and Ivy, his official cocoa greeters at Planes, Trains, and Automobiles.

According to the Chamber of Commerce, the buzz was positive, and they expected a big influx of shoppers. *Thank you, Giles.* He'd let her know that the shop owners had brought their prizes, and he'd put them in a big basket and covered it with a large clear cellophane bag.

Tomorrow evening would be the first display of Dickens Holiday of Lights. Shawn and Axel had run the mini train, going the full route and ensuring the lights and music worked perfectly.

She'd spent the past three days dealing with social media that had generated great interest. Messages had been sent to the center's website for reservations, and the seats were filled.

She hollered up the stairs, "We're leaving in five minutes! Don't forget your gloves."

Simone brushed against her leg, meowing. Elise picked up the cat and moved a hand slowly over her head, brushing her fingers over the feline's new pink collar. "You've already eaten, but I'll give you a couple of treats."

Giles had purchased a collar with a tracking device. The Cat Trac could be monitored through an app on their phones. At first, she'd protested that he'd gone to too much expense, but he'd felt it necessary to keep an eye on the cat, remembering the night Sophie had cried her heart out.

He'd certainly made an impact on their lives. A bouquet of flowers had arrived Wednesday, a thank-you for all her help at his open house. He'd made sure Sophie's favorite song played from his Christmas display. He'd attended her soccer game.

Her son had been ecstatic when he'd gotten a text from Giles with an image of the new menu he'd had printed displaying the custom logo. He was also going to have it added to the sign he was hanging in front of the store and painted in gold letters on the front window.

Giles's kindness always included the kids. He was really too good to be true.

Hurried footsteps coming down the stairs let her know the kids were on their way.

Emile shoved his arms into his jacket. "Mom, Hailey wants to help make the snowman for Mr. Giles."

"I'm sure it will be okay." She tugged Sophie's hat down a little more to cover the tops of her ears. "Remember, there will be a lot of people. No wandering off. Let's go."

Chapter 10

They'd come a little early to get a spot close to the tree. Aunt Britta had let Elise know the square would be crowded, with everyone wanting to attend the annual tree lighting. She recognized a number of familiar faces, but the visitors outnumbered the locals. The mayor had just given her annual welcome-to-Dickens speech, and the elementary school choir had crowded around the interior of the gazebo to sing a medley of holiday songs.

Vendors sold hot drinks and snacks from pushcarts, each decorated with colored lights. The mouthwatering smell of freshly made popcorn was the champion scent. The shops would reopen as soon as the mayor flipped the switch for the lights on the beautiful Norway spruce.

The Department of Public Works had decorated the beauty with silver and red ribbons, silver stars, angels, and red, gold, and blue balls.

"Like I said when we were at home, stay close to me." Elise curled her fingers tighter around Sophie's hand.

"Where did Emile go?" Giles asked.

"I had to be a big girl and accept my son is growing up. He and Hailey are with Jamie and the other Euphoria band members."

"I never expected it to be this crowded," Giles chuckled. "The excitement is as high as waiting for the tree lighting at Rockefeller Center."

"That's the giant tree in the book *The Carpenter's Gift*," Sophie said excitedly. "I wonder who is going to get a house made from the tree."

"Sophie, when your mom told me about the book you're reading, I was fascinated and did a little research. Since 2007, the Christmas trees have been transported to a mill and used by Habitat for Humanity. The lumber is stamped with the year of the tree lighting so the people who get the new home know the date of the tree that decorated Rockefeller Center."

Elise beamed a smile at Giles. "Thank you for sharing that. When I get enough money, I'd like to take the kids to New York to see the tree, even if it's just for one overnight."

If it were possible, the number of people eager to witness the tree lighting had grown, pushing them a little closer to the front.

"Mom, everyone is squishing me, and I can hardly see the star on the tree."

Elise decided it had been a mistake to get this close to the front. They'd be starting the countdown in a minute, and it would take many *pardon me*'s to get through this crowd.

"I know how you feel. When I was five years old, my parents took my brother and me to a tree lighting, and all I could see were the wide branches at the bottom of the tree. How much do you weigh?" Giles asked the young girl.

"Giles, you can't put her on your shoulders," Elise challenged.

"Why not? It won't be for long. How much does she weigh?"

Once again, he was thoughtful and kind. She relented and answered his question: "At her last checkup, she was fifty-nine pounds."

"I've carried a fifty-pound sack of potatoes, so I can handle an extra nine pounds. As soon as the mayor announces the countdown, I'll put her on my shoulders."

He settled his hands on Sophie's shoulder. "Get ready!"

The mayor stepped up to announce it was time to start the countdown, and Giles picked up her daughter and settled her on his shoulders. He locked his arms securely around her legs and hips.

"No wiggling around!" Elise warned her giggling daughter.

"Can you see better now?" Giles shouted above the cacophony of happy voices counting down.

"Yes!" she squealed, grabbing his head to hold on.

"Now, that's what I call getting up in the world." Elise put a hand on her daughter's back to support her. No one could put a price on the smile that filled her daughter's face.

A chorus of yays and clapping went up when the tree burst to life with thousands of twinkling lights. Sophie squealed again at seeing the star light up.

"It's so beautiful," Elise called above the clamor of surrounding revelers.

Giles lifted Sophie off his shoulders and took a deep breath. "Now, that wasn't so bad."

"Thanks, Mr. Giles!" Sophie gave him a big hug.

Axel, Freja, Holly, and Ivy made their way toward them. "Another successful tree lighting," Axel announced, slapping Axel on the back."As spectacular as Rockefeller Center!"

"Grandpa, you're in charge of the girls," Freja told Axel. "I'm helping Britta and Dane at the shop for a little while. I'll be back to help you, Lars, and Jens make our snowman for Planes, Trains, and Automobiles."

"Can we get popcorn and cider?" Holly asked, and the other girls chimed in.

"Please? Please?"

Elise couldn't fight the pleading look in her daughter's eyes. Before she could say she'd take the girls, Axel volunteered.

"I'll take them. I'll meet you at the snow-covered field surrounding Grosvenor's Pond, where we'll be making the snowmen."

Before she could say, "Okay," Axel's granddaughters took his hands and tugged him toward the popcorn wagon.

"I don't know whether to thank him or offer my sympathy." Elise laughed and turned her attention to Giles. "I don't know about you, but I could use a cup of coffee."

"What? You're not going to have hot chocolate, Dickens's official drink?" Giles teased. "I could use a cup, too."

Along with the coffee, they each got a freshly made churro. Due to the expected crowd, the street had been closed to vehicles. Their walk took them toward the gazebo, outlined with tiny white lights.

They paused near one of the benches that lined the walk. "Let's sit a minute," he suggested, taking a bite of his churro and nodding. "These are quite good. Madrid is the best place in the world to get a churro."

Elise shifted on the bench so she could face him. "You traveled all the way to Madrid for a churro?"

He chuckled lightly. "They make ones that are just as good at a little shop on Mulberry Street in New York. I frequented the place when I was going to school there and became good friends with the owner. He's passed his skills down to his children."

"You've had crepes in Paris and Marseille, crumpets in England, and churros in Madrid. You've seen the tree in Rockefeller Center."

"The best tea I've ever enjoyed was in India - a first-flush Darjeeling grown in the Himalayan foothills," he added with a smile.

"The gossip queens were right. You're a sophisticated world traveler. We must seem like country bumpkins to you. I borrowed teacups and teapots for our little get-together. I ordered the tea leaves online. Why are you giving all that up to live in a small town in New England?"

Their fun sparring had done an about-face. When he paled slightly, she realized, too late, how insultingly boorish she'd sounded. He'd never pretended to be better than anybody. He'd been nothing but kind. *What have you done? You like Giles a lot.*

She pressed her fingertips to his arm. "I'm sorry. That was a snobbish thing for me to say. I have no right to question why you want to change your lifestyle."

"You're right. It's my decision."

She expected him to get up and walk away, but he leaned close and kissed her on the tip of her nose.

"When we have more time, I'll let you know what influenced my life changes."

She lowered her head, unable to face him. "Life's changes happen when you least expect them. I have no right to take this out on you, but sometimes I get frustrated. I raise my children alone and do what I can to provide for them. We live in a house that needs a lot of work. I pray the furnace will last through the winter. Slate tiles are missing from the roof. You already know about the musical plumbing."

"Your children are quite happy. They're not starving, and you have support from family and a great group of friends. You love your job. Personally, I think your house is fun and unique. What haven't you told me?"

She buried her tightly gripped fingers in her lap. "My aunt and uncle are the only ones who know this, so please don't share. My husband and I were going to open our own restaurant. We'd been looking for the perfect location, and finally, this property went up for sale. We had just enough money to put down and submitted a bid, less than what the owner was asking. Then the realtor let us know there was another bidder who was willing to pay the full price."

He placed a hand over hers in her lap and squeezed lightly. "They outbid you."

"Yes, but it gets worse. The competitor upped their bid by ten percent. My husband was obsessed with getting the property. He found one of those illegal card games and tried to win additional money. He lost half of what we'd planned to put down and then took out a loan from, let's say, unsavory money lenders and lost that. He had a drinking problem and got behind the wheel when he'd had too much to drink and was killed in an accident."

"I'm so sorry, Elise."

"I knew nothing of this until a guy wearing a fancy suit showed up at my door asking for the money my husband borrowed."

"Did he produce any kind of paperwork?"

"No. I was stunned by what he told me, but I somehow managed to laugh in the guy's face. I told him I wasn't aware that my husband borrowed any money and that I wasn't responsible for his debt. I slammed the door in his face. I was too busy dealing with his death, my children's heartbreak, and wondering how we were going to survive financially. My husband handled all the finances and never told me he'd stopped paying the premiums for his life insurance. A week later, I got a letter informing me of my responsibility for my husband's debt. They offered to set up monthly payments with a thirty-five percent interest rate. They gave me thirty days to make the first payment."

"That's outrageous!"

"I decided we had to move and contacted my Aunt Britta and Uncle Dane. I worked for a small planning event center for two years and assisted my husband, Claude, at a French pastry shop. My aunt and uncle recommended me for the job at the event center and helped pay for our move. I'd inherited the house we were living in, but we'd taken out a mortgage. The house sold quickly, and I had just enough money for a down payment on the Ringing Rocks House. Since we moved, I haven't heard from the shyster money lenders, but I'm still frightened they'll track me down and demand payment."

She expelled a deep breath that froze in the night air. "That's our move-to-Dickens saga. I can't believe I told you all that. Thanks for listening."

"Any time. I admire you for all you've accomplished, and I like your house. I look forward to tapping on the rocks." He reached for her hands and cradled them between his, adding more warmth. "I wasn't going to say anything, but I think you need a good laugh. Plus, I've got a crazy theory."

"I'm surprised you're still being kind after the way I spoke to you,"

"That's what friends are for. I researched your house and found information at the County Historical Society. The house was built in 1855 and is referred to as the Ringing Rocks House. The rocks were transported from a quarry in Upper Black Eddy, Pennsylvania, which means those railroad tracks went back that far. Today, there's a park you can visit. According to the website, the rocks ring if you tap on them."

"I can't wait to tell the kids. Did you find out anything else?"

"Brace yourself. At one point, your house was a house of ill repute."

"A brothel!" Elise laughed out loud. "That's shockingly funny."

"It became a hotel in 1865, shortly after the Civil War. I didn't want to say anything until I did more research, but I think you might be able to prove Axel's claim that Charles Dickens visited the area. In 1867, he traveled through the Portland area on his way to New York."

"That means he might have stopped at our depot!"

"That's a great possibility. I'll bet the other part of the depot, with the beautiful tiles, was a 'parlor' where passengers could relax while traveling long distances and get some respite between trains. Other passengers took advantage of the hotel."

"That would make sense." In her excitement, Elise slid to the edge of the bench. "Are you saying Charles Dickens could have slept at my house?"

"The county posted a faded hotel register—no name of the hotel visible. The script is hard to read, but one name looks like C. Dickens. There's a partial, very faded date of 1867."

Giles paused and drank his warm coffee. "This is my problem. Your house has a historical background. The three troublemakers are part of the Historical Society and should know about buildings with unique histories. I found the information on your house quite easily. When you joined the society, did they talk about the significance of your house?"

"No. Half the time, they gossip. I'm fascinated by what you've told me. I've dropped the ball researching the history of the depot and the other half that will be the museum. I'll add researching Charles Dickens to my list."

"Those three know more than they're willing to share and have sat on information about the depot and your house. Wouldn't it be funny if one of those women was related to the brothel owner and that's why they're dead set against the center investigating the historical significance?"

"They would finally get their due, and Axel would get the last laugh." She leaned into him and put her head on his shoulder, feeling his cold coat against her cheek. "Thanks for making me feel better."

Giles stood and held out his gloved hand. "Now tell me what I'm supposed to do to make an award-winning snowperson."

Elise liked the feel of his larger hand around hers. "Each snowperson-making spot is marked with a name, and we have two hours to mold our creation."

"I have the mini crepes we made in a cooler in the car. I didn't forget Emile's original graphic of a snowman making crepes. We'll set the posterboard on an easel. When he showed it to me, I said something was missing. He kept staring at it until I said it was missing the logo he created for me."

"I attached a paintbrush to a long stick," Elise said, "so it will appear that our snowman painted the sign. I made the chef's hat for the snowman and the berets for the girls to wear. Shawn sent me a message this afternoon that he'll find us."

"We make a great team! Just out of curiosity, who are the judges?"

Elise raised a brow. "Viola, one of your biggest fans, Tom Gridley and Andy Doritt."

"You mean one of the madams?"

Elise gasped, unable to hold back her laughter. "You'd better not say that too loudly."

Giles couldn't ever remember being this cold, but two hours later, having rolled and patted mounds of snow, he was quite pleased with how Pierre had turned out. The girls had decided on his name since he was wearing a beret. They'd flipped a red scarf over his shoulder. The stack of felt crepes attached to the beret had a slight tilt, like the Leaning Tower of Pisa. He laughed out loud when Elise produced a black mustache with curled ends, giving Pierre a rakish Frenchman look.

The hostesses—Sophie, Holly and Ivy—passed out the crepes Giles had brought, which were gone in no time. He was glad to see that visitors took note of the caricature drawing of the snowman. Emile and Hailey kept running back and forth between Euphoria's entry and theirs. The teenager was obviously enjoying himself.

"Wow! When you said you were keeping your theme a secret, now I know why," Axel said as he and Freja joined them.

Holly and Ivy threw themselves against their grandparents. "Pop! Mama! We gave out all of the crepes. Can we go for hot chocolate?" Holly asked.

"In a minute," Freja said, wrapping her arms around both girls. "These two monkeys haven't stopped talking about their sleepover tonight. After the judging, we'll take Sophie with us. Karla will bring Lynnie to our house. We'll take the girls to the event center for *The Bells of St. Dickens* rehearsal tomorrow morning at ten o'clock."

"Sophie, too, hasn't stopped talking about the play," Elise said. "This will also be her first sleepover. They did a great job handing out the mini crepes. How are things with Casey Jones?"

"We left him in the capable hands of Lars and Jens. The judging will start in a few minutes, but we wanted to see how you were doing." Freja brushed her finger across the edge of a felt crepe. "I love this hat. People are all abuzz about the Cocoa Crawl and the train ride at the center tomorrow."

Axel kept his back to the girls and spoke directly to the adults. "Why do I get a bad feeling about tomorrow night? Those who shall not be named sabotaged Karla and Sebastian's show at the library annex."

"They were depending on wired power," Freja answered.

"That can't happen here. We're all set," Shawn said. "Mother Nature charged all the light sensors. Tomorrow, I'll dust off any residual snow and double-check the connections to the sensors and timers."

Giles held out a hand. "Thanks, Shawn, for helping tonight. We couldn't have done it without you."

"I had a lot of fun. Judging is going to start soon, and I'm going to check out the competition,"

Shawn said. “I’ll join you before they announce the winners.”

“Let me take the girls for hot chocolate,” Freja volunteered. “See you in the winner’s circle.”

Emile came running over, smiling and out of breath. “Has anyone said anything more about my drawing?”

“You’ve got a winner. The drawing got more attention than Pierre.” Giles gave him a high five. “You should make him part of your candy monster squad—the marshmallow dude who’s just been fire-roasted to make a s’more.”

“Mr. Giles, that’s a bussin’ idea. I’ll do it!” Emile turned to Elise. “Mom, can I go ice skating with the band and Hailey after the awards?”

“Are there skates to rent? What time will you be home?”

“Yes, they rent them, and I have my own money. Jamie’s father will be there and bring me home by midnight. Please? It will be a lot of fun.”

“Time to put on your big-girl pants,” Giles teased Elise.

“Okay, but be careful,” she said to Emile.

“Thanks, Mom. Mr. Giles. See you later!”

The teenagers ran off, and Giles looked around. Spectators were looking at the snow people. He took advantage of being alone with Elise for a few minutes before the judges arrived. “Thanks again for helping me. You must be tired, and tomorrow is a big day.”

Elise expelled a heavy sigh. "Emile, Hailey, and I will be serving hot chocolate to the customers who come to 2 Sisters, but I'll be at the event center by two p.m. I'm bringing food for the kids when rehearsal is over. We've set up a Christmas movie marathon to keep them busy until the first train ride. All the reservations are filled. The teenagers who normally work at the event center will be working, too."

How she could keep straight who, what, where and when was beyond his thinking. "You can count on me to help. Consider it payback for helping me the other night."

"No payback is needed. Thanks to you, we'll be able to have the light show. Have you had any luck getting a new pastry chef?"

"No," he replied, shaking his head. "My employment ad hasn't generated a response. Lars, Jens, and Freja reached out to their baking contacts and hit a dead end."

Elise wrapped her arms around her waist and shifted back and forth. "What are you going to do?"

Giles slowly ran his hands up and down her arms. "I'd give you a hug to warm you, but that might raise too many eyebrows. I'll work by myself. I'll limit the number of selections and prep the fillings ahead of time, just like I did for my open house."

"It still bothers me that the guy you hired had bottom-feeder integrity, leaving you high and dry. Other than the train ride next weekend and the play on Christmas Eve, we have no events scheduled. The train club is handling visitors and tours of the train displays, so I'm not needed. Until you get someone, I can give you a hand for the lunch crowd, but not dinner."

"I'll accept your help only if you let me pay you—no argument."

"Okay. I'll splurge on something extra for the kids for Christmas."

"Again, I don't know how to thank you." He glanced away and reluctantly lowered his arms. "Here come the judges."

The three judges, each wearing a large button on their coat that read Judge, stood back to assess the full presentation. Tom Gridley and Andy Dorrit bore big smiles as they slowly walked around Chef Pierre, making notations on their clipboards. Giles was surprised when he didn't get a gushy hello from Viola.

"Sorry I couldn't make the open house," Andy said to Giles. "My wife couldn't stop raving about the crepes. We'll be having dinner when you open."

"The Frenchman theme and painting are quite clever and great advertising for your new shop," Tom mentioned. "We're busy at the tree farm, but we'll visit you when the season ends. After that, we'll have time to work on our plans for the Dickens Historical Evergreen Preserve."

"Who knows? One of your trees might stand tall in Rockefeller Center someday," Giles said.

"The book my daughter, Sophie, is reading mentions that the young boy planted a pinecone to start his tree. Do you bury a pinecone?" Elise asked.

"Trees really aren't started from a pinecone," Tom explained. "There are seeds inside the pinecones, so when the cone opens up, the seeds fall out. We have our own beds. Trees are started in the wilds by wind, rain, birds, and squirrels."

Viola made additional notes on her clipboard before interrupting their conversation. "Are you all set for tomorrow?" she asked Elise.

"The Dickens Holiday of Lights at the depot? Absolutely!"

The biddy's back stiffened. "No. I'm talking about the Cocoa Crawl. Under my direction, the Chamber of Commerce has gone all out to promote the day and next weekend. We're counting on this new idea to bring in many shoppers."

"Viola, I'm sure everyone is aware of your efforts, and they'll pay off," Giles schmoozed, trying to remain as patient as possible.

The judges stayed a few more minutes before heading for the Christmas tree, where the winner of the snowman-making contest would be announced.

Elise remained quiet until the judges moved on. "I don't trust that woman. She's acting like the Cocoa Crawl was all her idea. No matter what we've done, she's against the depot and its historical significance."

The spectators had moved to stand in front of the beautifully lit tree, with all heads turned away from them. He turned to Elise, pulled her into his arms, and was pleased when she returned his embrace.

"I still say she's got something to hide. Now, let's get our award. No matter what, between us, we've won first prize." He kissed her once and went back for a second that lasted a little longer, heightening the warmth of their kiss.

"No matter how grumpy I am, you can raise me up," she sighed. "With those warm, prize-winning kisses, does that mean we get first-and second-place awards?"

"Minx." He chuckled and tightened his arm about her waist.

They found Axel, Freja, Sebastian, Karla, and Shawn, along with the kids, close to the gazebo. Mayor Elizabeth McKenzie stepped to the podium. In her hand was a small trophy shaped like a snowman.

"Thank you all for coming this evening. The judges said this was the most challenging snowman competition they've ever had to judge. One point separates the first and second-place winners, but we have a tie for second place. Congratulations, Jamie Nielson and the band Euphoria, for the second year in a row. The second-place winners are Casey Jones and Pierre the Frenchman."

Everyone cheered, but Jamie and his band's boisterous cheering drowned out the clapping.

Axel shook hands with Giles. "Congratulations. Your theme was really good."

"Right back at you. The 'finishing touches' were Elise's ideas. I know Pierre has to stay, but do we take our displays with us?"

"I'd like to say everyone is trustworthy, but take your stuff," Axel advised. "See you tomorrow."

"Sophie, before you run off." Elise hugged and kissed her. "Behave. I'll see you at the event center tomorrow."

Elise blinked rapidly, trying to erase the tears from her eyes. Giles draped a comforting arm around her shoulders. "Are you okay?"

She nodded quickly and sniffed. "This is the first time she's sleeping away from me. My mom's ego is saying she'll miss me, get homesick, and Karla will call me to come and get Sophie."

"I think she'll be having too much fun to get homesick. From the short amount of time I've spent with those girls, we should have a little sympathy for Axel and Freja."

"You're right. Thanks for chasing my blues away again. Let's collect Pierre's painting and the easel."

The excited chatter that filled the car on the way to the tree lighting was absent on the way home. Giles couldn't be more pleased with how the evening had turned out. Experiencing grand openings of his restaurants took a back seat to the happiness he'd enjoyed tonight. The beautiful woman sitting in the passenger seat was largely responsible. And the wonderful evening wasn't over.

They were a couple of miles from the house when he said, “I know you’re tired, but I have a little surprise for you.”

“If it takes building another snowman, I’ll pass,” she returned with a short laugh.

“No. Relaxing and looking at the stars are requirements.”

“Now you have me intrigued.”

They pulled into his driveway. “My surprise is behind the house.”

Stepping out of the car, they were immediately enveloped in the cold night air. They followed the path he’d shoveled that afternoon. The sky overhead was clear, with millions of stars, just what he was hoping for. He pulled out his phone and pressed a button, and she gasped when they walked into his yard.

“Giles! An igloo?”

The clear plastic-domed tent came with tiny white lights in the seams and encircled the dome.

“This is amazing! When did you set this up?”

“This afternoon. Don’t laugh, but I followed the directions, and it was quite easy.” He unzipped the arched front panel, and they stepped inside. He turned on an electric heater in the shape of an old-fashioned potbelly stove. “It will be warm in a few minutes.”

Elise grinned, turning in a circle. “This is amazing. You have a telescope, four camp chairs and a table. All the comforts of home.”

"I thought the kids would enjoy looking at the stars, too." He walked over to a cooler, removed a bottle of chilled wine, and set a platter of crackers and cheese on the round table in the center of the chairs. "I had drinks for the kids, too. I didn't know what you liked to drink, so I selected a Chardonnay to go with the Gouda, Monterey Jack, Butterkäse, and the baby Swiss."

"Now you're an expert on pairing cheese with wine."

Giles hesitated before pouring the wine into the glasses he'd set on the table. "Elise, you're doing it again. I went online to see which cheeses would go the best with Chardonnay."

"I'm sorry. It's not your fault. My late husband overindulged in wine, so I haven't had any in quite a while."

"I'm sorry if I've made you feel uncomfortable." He moved to the cooler and lifted the lid. "I have iced tea and canned soda."

"No. I'd enjoy a glass. This is absolutely perfect." She took a sip before placing a few slices of cheese and crackers on her plate. "Now you're interested in the stars."

The dome started to warm up, and he removed his jacket. "Actually, I've always been interested in the weather but never had time to pursue a hobby. I love looking at the stars, especially in the winter."

She removed her jacket and draped it around the back of her chair. “What is the brightest star in the winter sky?”

He moved to the telescope and set the focus on the northern sky. “Sirius is the brightest star in the constellation Canis Major, in the northern hemisphere.” He shifted the eyepiece in her direction. “Take a look.”

Giles reached for his cell phone to add a little music to the relaxing atmosphere. If a slow dance happened to come on…

“Wow! It seems so close! You want to reach out and touch it!” She gave him the biggest smile. “The kids will love looking through this telescope.”

As Don McClean started singing, “Starry, starry night,” the first words of the song “Vincent,” Giles held out his arms.

“Only if you want to dance,” he invited.

Elise hesitated for a few seconds but stepped into his arms. She wrapped hers around his waist, and he rested his cheek atop her head. They moved slowly to the beautiful song.

“I’m sure Emile would appreciate knowing that the lyrics to this song represent the life, work, and death of Vincent van Gogh. The lyrics refer to *The Starry Night*, one of the famous paintings of the Dutch Postimpressionist.”

“Giles, you’re full of surprises and the most unboring person I’ve ever met.” She sighed heavily and tightened her arms.

"I'll take that as a compliment." He buried his cheek a little deeper into the soft weave of her hat. The song ended, and Stephen Sanchez started singing "Until I Found You." Giles wanted to tighten his arms, but his conscience reminded him he was a fraud. He'd found Elise for all the wrong reasons, but his heart had taken over. He was falling in love with her.

The song ended, and she lowered her arms before stepping back. "I haven't danced in a very long time. All this has been wonderful, but it's time for this Cinderella to end the night."

"Don't bother leaving a slipper. I know where to find you," he teased. "I'll walk you home and then come back and shut things down."

She put on her coat. "Not necessary. Thank you again for a lovely end of the day. Giles, you're too good to be true." She initiated a very soft kiss but backed away before he could take her in his arms.

No, I'm not. "I'll see you at the Dickens Depot tomorrow night after I award the gift basket." He unzipped the door opening. "Night."

Sadness filled his heart as he watched her walk away. Things had certainly taken a turn in a direction he'd never anticipated or intended. How much longer could he keep the truth from her?

Chapter 11

Since Elise was alone in her office, no one saw her yawn for the third time. She'd had a bad night's sleep with Sophie at a sleepover, having anticipated that the phone would ring. The last time she'd looked at the clock was four a.m. She texted Karla a little after eight a.m. and asked how she'd survived the night. She came back with, *Ha! Ha! They actually slept and are eating homemade waffles for breakfast.* She wrote that she'd have them at the event center a little after ten a.m. for play rehearsal.

A few minutes later, Sophie called and said she missed her mother but was having fun and wanted to invite the girls for a sleepover at their house. So much for being a worrywart.

Elise brought the makings for hero subs for lunch and sat with the girls while they ate. All of them jabbered happily at once, and she got a good idea of what Karla's night had been like. After lunch, she spent time with the kids watching *Elf,* then headed for her office.

She updated the winter visiting hours for the train museum and double-checked the number of visitors who had signed up for tonight's train ride in case there were any cancellations. Elise looked away from her computer when Shawn rushed into her office in a frenzy. His steamed-up look let her know something was very wrong.

"My gut instinct says someone tampered with the lights," Elise blurted.

Shawn paced in front of her desk. "I just finished double-checking the connections, and Axel was right when he suggested someone wanted our event not to happen. Someone unplugged the light sensors on two dozen displays and laid them facedown so they couldn't charge in the sun. I sent a message to Axel as soon as I found the first one."

"Who would be so spiteful?" She'd eaten only half a sub, but now it felt like a boulder in her stomach. "I'd better put together a message to let everyone know the show is canceled. The kids will be so disappointed."

Shawn perched on the corner of her desk and gave her a smile. "I wouldn't be so quick about doing that. We're still on. If the culprit had done their homework, they would have known that a standard solar battery can store energy from one to five days. We have a smaller battery, but the charge is good for at least three days."

Axel hurried in, drawing their attention. The anger on his face said it all. "I knew things were going too smoothly! This is the first time I've been able to get away. The Cocoa Crawl is a huge success. Planes, Trains, and Automobiles were busier than ever."

"This morning, I worked with Jamie and Ashley at 2 Sisters handing out hot cocoa, and we were super busy, too," Elise said. "I arrived at the event center a little before two o'clock and was surprised by the number of cars in the parking lot. The holiday train display is having a successful day."

"How are we on the lights?" Axel asked Shawn.

"We should be okay. As I explained to Elise, if the culprit had done their homework, they would have known that a standard solar battery could store energy from one to five days. Our charge is good for at least three days. They weren't very bright and left a trail of footsteps like Hansel and Gretel's breadcrumbs. I reconnected the lights and turned the sensors toward the sun."

"That makes me feel a whole lot better." Axel ran his fingers through his hair. "I just thought of something else. If they're that desperate, they might have damaged the tracks connected to the building where we keep the trains. I'm heading there now."

"I'll join you," Shawn said hurriedly.

Much relieved, she'd barely sat at her desk when her cell rang. Giles, the person who made her smile.

"How are things going in town?" Elise asked.

"Busier than ever, but you won't be happy with this latest gossip. Someone started a rumor that the Dickens Holiday of Lights has been canceled for this evening. They're saying there's a problem with the lights and that shoppers should spend more time in town."

Her temper was back in full force. "Someone tampered with the lights, but Shawn caught it in time, so the light show is still on. I didn't think whoever did this would go that far!"

While still on the phone, she checked the message requests for the event center. Ten were to confirm whether the show had been canceled. "I'm getting calls already. I'll send out a group email to the people who signed up for this evening to let them know the event is still on."

"I can put a flyer together here, but I'll need help passing them out."

"Giles, raising a teenager has opened my eyes to a whole new way of communication. I'll send a group message to Emile and Jamie to spread the word to their friends. They'll flood social media with the news that the Dickens Holiday of Lights show is still on for those who have signed up. I'll also put a message on our Facebook and Instagram pages."

"You do your thing, and I'll do mine. I'm on my way to Doritt's Diner. We'll squash the rumor from the hot spot for gossip. As soon as I give the winner their raffle basket this evening, I'll be out there to help. Please text me Emile's cell number."

"That's a great idea. Thanks for letting me know. See you later."

She posted a message on the website's home page, Facebook and Instagram. Emile and Jamie responded immediately. They were all meeting Mr.

Giles at his shop and would start posting. Crisis averted.

She needed some fresh air but grabbed her phone just in case.

The cold air attacked her cheeks the moment she stepped outside. She wrapped her wool scarf tighter around her neck and shoved her gloved hands into her pockets. The sun was dipping toward the western sky, which was clear of any threat of snow. The number of cars in the parking lot had dwindled. The museum would be shutting down in a half hour.

She headed for the depot and walked up the snow-cleared path to it, but her eyes were drawn to the gazebo at the curve of the tracks that would be the start of the ride into the nearby woods.

Tonight wouldn't have happened, disappointing many children, if Giles hadn't let her know about the vicious rumor. How many times had she asked herself over the past few weeks who Giles DeLuc was, her veritable knight in shining armor?

Dancing with him last evening in the igloo had been one of the nicest evenings she'd spent in a very long time. And he hadn't thought of doing something nice just for her. There had been four chairs, and he'd thought of having drinks for her children.

Thinking back, she knew her marriage hadn't been a bed of roses. Her mother said marriage required a lot of understanding and acceptance, but it had to work both ways. Claude had always been about himself. She was the one who'd made concessions and excuses for him for the sake of their children.

Their marriage had been on shaky ground, and she'd thought having a child would bring them closer together. He'd been happy when they'd had a son. Emile would carry on the family name and follow in Claude's footsteps as a pâtissier. He hadn't been pleased when she'd become pregnant with Sophie and had begun to pull away from her. He'd had very little to do with the children. She'd considered leaving him and moving to Georgia to live with her aunt and uncle, but marriage meant understanding and acceptance.

Thinking more about what she'd had with Claude, she realized it had all been one-sided. She deserved more for herself and her children.

She had just met Giles but could see the difference between him and her late husband. Was she wrong to make comparisons? If and when she ever fell in love again, she'd make sure the give-and-take in their relationship was on both sides. Thinking about a future relationship had to take a back seat right now.

She opened the depot door to ensure everything was ready for this evening. Long wooden benches were spaced throughout the room. The original potbelly stove had been converted to propane, retaining the aesthetics of an old-fashioned depot.

A glass-fronted counter designated the area where visitors waiting for the train could purchase hot chocolate, soft drinks, and freshly made popcorn. Leslie's Bakes and More had delivered trays of chocolate chip and sugar cookies shaped like steam trains, all individually sealed in cellophane bags. Her aunt and uncle had also made fudge shaped like a train engine.

She had a few minutes before returning to the event center. She unlocked the door to the other side of the depot and turned on the lights. Now that she'd talked about the space with Giles, she could picture the room being used as a respite for weary travelers. If there were some way to prove Charles Dickens had stopped here, they could finally end the debate about the historical value of the building. The cherry on top would be if she could prove that Dickens had stayed at her house.

Enough time for wishes, she decided and locked the door—time to get ready for this evening.

Her cell indicated an incoming text from Emile. *Jamie and Euphoria met up at Mr. Giles's creperie so we could flood social media. He treated us to pizza. Jamie and the band are coming together, so you can give them their assignments for this evening. I'm riding with Mr. Giles to the depot. Mom, I like him. He's a cool guy.*

Okay, see you later.

Giles was a nice guy, she thought, but was he for real?

The butterflies in her stomach were going crazy as excitement built. She stood inside the depot and checked off the assignments for the evening. The kids showed up a half hour early to get their assignments. Considering they worked the regular shows, they knew how important this evening was and wore their event center vests.

Three kids would work the concession, and Jamie would work the ticket booth, confirming reservations. To alleviate any confusion, Ashley handed out colored wristbands stamped with the departure time.

Elise checked her watch before addressing the kids. "This is a big night for the depot, and thanks so much for working this evening. You'll keep the same assignments for next Saturday, too."

She looked directly at Jamie and Ashley. "There will be six rides. People are going to show up wanting a ride, but they have to show their reservation confirmation on their phone or a printed copy. Their assigned time is on their ticket. If anyone has any problems or questions, send them to me or Jamie's father. Does anyone have any questions?"

"Will we be able to ride the train?" Emile asked, standing beside Hailey.

"Absolutely. You'll get your ride after everyone leaves. I plan to join you. Before we open the event, all of you help yourselves to a drink and a cookie."

The door opened, and Giles, Axel, Sebastian, and Shawn walked in. Axel and Shawn wore official engineer caps. Sebastian had asked Giles to act as a conductor to assist people on and off the train if needed. Both wore hard-sided conductor caps.

"The timers are set to go on in five minutes," Shawn announced, looking at the kids. "Come out to the platform, and we'll have an official countdown for the light displays."

They stepped outside. Karla was pushing a baby carriage, and the four girls were walking beside Freja. They were all bundled up with warm coats, hats, scarves, and gloves.

"The whole gang is here!" Elise announced, giving Sophie a quick hug before her daughter rejoined her friends. Her big smile said it all.

"This is like another tree lighting," Giles declared, standing beside her.

"Pray they all come on," she said for his ears alone.

Axel took center stage and held up a large trainman's watch. "Here we go!"

Elise gripped Giles's hand when they started counting backward. Ten seconds later, the world brightened, creating a winter wonderland. The girls screamed, clapped, and jumped up and down, and a different kind of excitement filled Elise's body.

The gazebo commanded the center, with a beautifully lit tree and the smaller displays closer to the tracks. Christmas music filled the area.

Giles winked at Elise. “The gazebo looks magnificent. What happened to Charles Dickens?”

Elise gently poked him in the side with her elbow. “Very funny. Let’s just say he missed the train.”

“Time for me to get behind the engine and drive her to the depot. Shawn will be riding shotgun,” Axel announced.

Freja threw her arms around her husband and gave him a big hug. “This is a dream come to life for you. It’s even more beautiful than I imagined.”

“Mommy! When can we go on the train?” Sophie asked.

“You four are on the first train out, front car, along with Mrs. Frost and Mrs. Nielson. Go inside and get your wristbands.”

“Do you need me to do anything?” Freja asked.

“Keep an eye on the girls.”

A line of cars was already pulling into the parking lot. “Here we go!”

Puffs of steam shot up from the round smokestack as the engine slowly made its way to the depot, pulling small passenger cars. Each car accommodated twenty riders, and the caboose was just for show. Each ride took twenty minutes. Riders were told the interiors weren’t heated, but small lap robes would be provided.

Elise closely monitored what was happening between the depot and the platform. The children and their parents' wide-eyed reactions to seeing the lights and the unique steam engine were worth all the work and worry they'd gone through.

People who hadn't purchased a ticket came to see the lights. They weren't allowed to follow the tracks beyond the depot area but were pleased by what they saw. Quite a few had reserved their spot for next week but couldn't wait that long to see the display.

Giles jumped right in, helping kids and adults on and off the train. In Elise's mind, everything was going very smoothly. The concession stand did a big business. They'd put a sign by the register explaining the sales went into a scholarship fund they maintained for children who couldn't afford to pay for dancing school lessons or musical instrument rentals and lessons. Toy donation boxes were overflowing.

When the last train ride of the evening pulled into the depot, Elise watched the passengers get off and braced herself when she saw Viola headed in her direction. She was accompanied by a man and a woman with three young children. The parents took the children to the depot.

"Elise, the Dickens Holiday of Lights was very enjoyable. My grandchildren loved the ride and the beautiful displays in the woods. You went all out designing the depot's interior to make it look authentic."

If someone had stuck her with a pin, they wouldn't have gotten any blood. Maybe Christmas was a season of miracles. "Thank you. I'm so happy you enjoyed the ride."

"I believe we had a win-win day. The Cocoa Crawl was an overwhelming success. Next week will be even busier, as it's the last shopping weekend before Christmas. Now I'll join my family."

Giles came out of the depot with two cups in his hands. "I got the last of the hot chocolate. Cookies, popcorn, and fudge are gone. I must have dirt on my face. Viola walked right past me and didn't say a word."

"We're going to get a blizzard," she uttered, accepting the cup. "She's pleased with the turnout for the Cocoa Crawl and anticipates next week will be even more successful. She also told me how much she enjoyed the train ride and liked how I designed the depot's interior to make it look authentic."

"Who was that woman?" Giles hesitated for a moment. "If she's pleased with the day's events, maybe she wasn't the one responsible for trying to sabotage the lights.'

"Unless her children's happiness made her feel guilty for objecting so much. If it wasn't her, then who was?"

"That's an excellent question. I have a problem with her comment that you designed the inside to 'make it *look* authentic.' That tells me she still doesn't believe the depot has historical value. We should've had that hologram of Charles Dickens getting on the train."

"I won't let her tongue-in-cheek compliment rain on my parade." Elise held up her cup so they could tap rims. "Here's to the Dickens Depot Express. Tonight was wonderful. We'll be leaving for our train ride in a few minutes. The girls will be having their second ride, too."

"I had a great time. The feedback from the passengers when they got off was overwhelmingly positive. The kids mentioned they want a Polar Express ride so they can wear their pajamas."

"We'd need heat in the cars, but I'll add it to the list for next year. Thank you again for your help." She tapped the brim of his conductor's hat. "You look cute. Are you available to do this again next week?"

"Absolutely. I had a great time. I put out feelers to the shop owners to let me know if they were still busy, even with the train ride. People stayed after the Cocoa Crawl prize was awarded. Feedback was that it was a great idea, and visitors discovered shops they hadn't been to before."

"Thanks to you for suggesting the idea. Now, it's our turn to ride the train."

Chapter 12

Monday morning, Giles sat at his desk in his office, which was a little larger than a storage closet. His corporate office had been at the top of a ten-story building with two walls of windows overlooking neighboring skyscrapers in Chicago. An executive assistant had kept him focused on his hectic life, and his driver had gotten him where he was supposed to be on time. Not having to drive had given him time to conduct business from the back seat. On his desk had been a yellow legal pad and a laptop.

He glanced out the window of his new office overlooking a parking lot, where he could see his SUV. When he'd gotten home from the holiday light show last night, he hadn't put his car in the garage and had had to clean off the half inch of snow that had fallen overnight. He'd pushed a snow shovel up and down the driveway while waiting for the car's heat to come up. He'd used up the last of his deicer and made a mental note to get more.

Did he miss corporate demands and having things done for him? No.

Earlier, he'd stopped at Doritt's Diner for coffee and a breakfast sandwich. By nine in the morning, every seat had been filled. Familiar faces had called out, “Good morning.” He’d gotten into a conversation with a few people. They thought the Dickens light show was beautiful, and that Axel and Sebastian should think about doing something like that for other holidays. Others had said how much fun they’d had doing the Cocoa Crawl.

He’d become one of them in a short time, and it was a great feeling. Giving of himself had come so naturally. The old, think-only-of-himself, career-driven Giles was gone—but he still had something to confess to the woman he’d fallen in love with. There was no doubt in his mind that he loved her. It had happened when he wasn’t looking, but he couldn’t share these feelings with her. She’d never believe him. Her wonderful children had worked their way into his heart, too.

Maybe he should have told her from the beginning who he was and why he’d moved to Dickens, but it was too late now.

Focusing on tomorrow demanded all his attention. The creperie’s waitresses, Toni and Melanie Dwyer, were coming in early to set up the tables. He’d show them where he kept the supplies and explain what was expected of them. The sisters had worked at their family restaurant in Bangor. They’d decided to sell the business when their father passed away. Their late father’s estate included a two-family Victorian house a block from Axel and Sebastian. Giles’s job opening had come at the perfect time for them.

Toni left a message on his cell last evening and gave him the name of a friend she thought would be perfect for the assistant chef job. Lyndsay Barnes was forty-one, single, and had been a close friend of the Dwyer sisters since grade school. They'd kept in touch even after Lyndsay had moved to New York to attend culinary school. She was currently not working and had plans to relocate.

He immediately called the woman, who had agreed to a Zoom interview this morning. He booted up his laptop and opened the meeting link. She was already waiting.

"Good morning, Lyndsay. Thanks for agreeing to this meeting on short notice."

Her long blond hair, which she'd pushed behind her ears, had a center part. She wore small gold ball earrings. Her eyes were a soft gray, and her only makeup was deep pink lipstick.

"Good morning. You mentioned that the position needs to be filled immediately."

"I reviewed the résumé you emailed. You're more than qualified, so naturally, that prompts several questions."

"I'm aware my background warrants a higher position, but I'm ready for a change."

Giles wasn't about to be burned again, so he was straight with this candidate. "I understand, but I want to be perfectly honest with you. I hired another chef, and he bailed at the last minute, accepting a higher-paying offer from a prestigious company. This may not be a 'glamorous' position, but I need someone who will make a real commitment and show up every day. Forty hours a week, but some hours are prep time. Right now, I'm open five days a week for lunch and dinner—closed on Sundays and Mondays. If you have no problem with any of that, we'll continue with this interview."

"I respect that you're being truthful with me. I wouldn't have agreed to this interview if I wasn't interested."

"Good enough. Lyndsay, tell me about yourself."

"As my résumé states, I attended Le Cordon Bleu in Paris and the Culinary Institute of America at Hyde Park. After graduation, I worked as a sous-chef under the head chef at an executive corporate cafeteria. When she got sick, everything was dumped into my lap. The company's president was very particular and expected his tastes to be catered to. When he retired, he offered me the personal chef position, including a private suite in his estate home."

"Did he have food allergies, or was he just particular about what he enjoyed?"

"No allergies or special diet requirements. He was in his eighties, but I made sure his dietary needs were healthy and well-rounded. I also prepared his meals on his yacht and private plane when he traveled worldwide. He jokingly said I was the only one who cared if he lived or died."

"What happened to your client?" At that question, he caught a watery film covering her gray eyes. That told him she cared about the man she worked for.

"He passed away three months ago." She blinked a few times, trying to clear her eyes. "Giles, Mr. DeLuc, please keep what I am about to share with you confidentially."

"Absolutely."

"He left his substantial estate to me. I was shocked. We'd become close friends, and I'd grown quite fond of him. He said I was the daughter he never had. His niece and nephew, who never came to see him, received five hundred dollars each. They contested the will, but it was ironclad. As you might surmise, I don't have to work a day in my life, but that's not me. I live a simple life without any extravagance."

Giles, too, had a hefty bank account, but that wasn't who he was now.

She gave him a little smile. "He was of French descent and loved crepes. They were a big part of his diet. I created several special recipes that I can share."

"You're more than qualified, and you've got the job. I'm always open to new recipes."

"That sounds wonderful, and I'd love to work for you."

"My official opening is tomorrow. When can you start?"

"I'm meeting with my lawyers in Chicago tomorrow to set up several trusts. I can be in Dickens by Wednesday evening to start work Thursday morning. Toni and Melanie mentioned they have a two-family house, and I plan to rent the vacant apartment."

"That will work. I have help tomorrow and Wednesday. I'll email you a letter confirming your hire and listing the hours. You can fill out the standard paperwork when you get here. You have my cell. Please keep in touch."

"I will. Now I have a question for you. Are you related to Ronald DeLuc?"

Apparently, she was well informed, he decided. "Ron was my brother."

"I hope this question doesn't get me fired before I start work. You and your brother own world-renowned five-star restaurants around the country. I was in his company several times. Why did you give it all up to establish a creperie in a small town?"

"I trust your silence. Like you, I needed to simplify my life after my brother passed away. Giving it all up and moving to Dickens is the best and smartest move I've ever made. The town is quaint, and the people are friendly. You'll love living and working here."

"It sounds like exactly what I'm looking for. Thanks for the job. I'll see you Thursday morning."

He ended the call, knowing the company she had worked for before the retired executive had hired her away. Its corporate headquarters had been in Chicago, and it had held events at Giles's flagship restaurant. Hopefully, his new hire had no connection to his former sister-in-law. Lyndsay had emailed a list of references, but time was of the essence, and he needed her help right now.

He had a full day of work preparing the crepe fillings, but first, he wanted to let Elise know he had hired an assistant.

Rather than text her, he called.

"Good morning, sunshine."

"Good morning to you, too. Have you looked outside? Snow clouds are hovering."

"All I have to do is think about your lovely face, and I'm filled with sunshine."

"Wow. Did you add happy juice to your coffee this morning?"

"No," he replied with a little chuckle. "I just hired an assistant pastry chef, but she can't start until Thursday morning."

"Oh, Giles. I'm so happy for you. Is she married?"

"She's single. Jealous?"

"No," she adamantly replied but followed with, "Maybe a little."

"Don't worry. My heart is spoken for." He realized what he'd admitted too late but quickly added, "I'm looking forward to attending the holiday concert at the high school this evening. I get to see Sebastian and the kids perform."

"Dinner is included at my house, at five. Emile's choice—homemade manicotti with meat sauce and Italian bread."

"Sounds delicious. I'll bring chocolate crepes for dessert, Emile's favorite. See you later this afternoon."

The happy feeling he was experiencing convinced him more and more he'd made the right decision to move to Dickens. He loved that Elise was jealous of Lyndsay, but their budding relationship would never become a bouquet. He'd wait until he got through the grand opening before he told her the truth. He started to put his cell phone in his back pocket but hesitated when a text popped up.

His happy mood died when he read the message from his former sister-in-law. *Call me ASAP. There's a major problem with the property purchased for the new restaurant.*

No way was he calling her. She'd created the problem, and she'd have to clear up the mess herself. He hit delete.

"Time to prepare for opening day."

Elise decided her children had one-track minds when it came to eating. This morning, she'd asked her son what he'd like for a special dinner, and he'd said manicotti with her meat sauce. Maybe she could also make an antipasto with extra salami and her Italian bread.

Making his special choice would not be a problem since manicotti was a variation of crepes.

Her kitchen smelled of fresh garlic and basil from her meat sauce. The pasta, stuffed with ricotta and mozzarella cheese, was rolled and lined up in the dish. All she had to add was the meat sauce and mozzarella topping. The bread dough was rising in a bowl on the back of the stove. The antipasto was in the refrigerator, covered with clear wrap. Giles was bringing dessert, so dinner was done.

She glanced at the clock and noted she had an hour before the school bus dropped the kids off in front of the house. The chair next to the potbelly stove was calling her name.

She picked up her cup of tea and made herself comfortable, curling her legs under her. She sighed, appreciating the quiet solitude. Her house was old and made noise but offered a warm, cozy feeling.

The first weekend of the light show had been a huge success, but she was already working on arrangements for next week. After going to the food store for the ingredients she'd needed for tonight's dinner, she'd stopped at Leslie's Bakes and More to order cookies. The owner said customers had mentioned what a great time they'd had at the light show. The Cocoa Crawl had brought in so many more customers. Cookies and brownies had been the biggest sellers. Leslie said she planned to double the amount for next week.

Then Elise stopped at 2 Sisters Kringle and Fudge. The three temporary employees who worked during the holidays were assisting customers. They acknowledged her with a wave, and she headed for the back. The major activity was in the baking and fudge-making kitchen. Freja had been making kringle with Lars and Jens while her aunt and uncle had been busy making fudge.

They, too, had given her more feedback on the weekend. Everyone's response had been positive, and they'd been making extra fudge for an upsurge of holiday shoppers on Saturday. Freja had already informed the extra help that Britta and Dane would be leaving the shop early Saturday evening. Elise had suggested to Axel and Sebastian that they have another family and employee train ride to enjoy the lights one more time to celebrate a successful event.

She cradled the mug in her hand and took another sip of cranberry-orange herbal tea. The weekend had been great, but Giles had made it that much more special. He was an enigma who had come into their lives like a fast-moving storm, but he was still here, ensconced in their lives when the dust settled. She hadn't been looking for loving warmth and companionship from the opposite sex, but he'd slowly brought out all her womanly feelings and emotions. Her children adored him.

What was holding her back from accepting that her feelings for him were turning into love? It had to be Giles—who was the opposite of Claude—and was too good to be true. Thoughtful, kind, considerate, generous… Was she jumping to conclusions by adding *loving*? She made a silent bet with herself that he'd show up this evening with flowers.

Enough daydreaming. She shoved up from the chair, anticipating a few knocks and whistles when she took a quick shower. She loved this house.

A little before five o'clock, she'd just finished setting the table when the front doorbell rang. The children had been overjoyed when she'd told them Giles would be joining them for dinner.

Sophie came running down the stairs. "It's Mr. Giles. I'll let him in."

Elise walked into the living room to see her daughter opening the door. A silent smile bloomed inside. He was carrying one of the most beautiful poinsettia plants she'd ever seen. *Score!* He was also carrying an oversized gift bag.

He hadn't bothered to button the front of his black fleece jacket. No jeans this evening. Dark gray dress trousers with a black and white argyle wool sweater. He also wore black leather boots. He looked good. Really good.

"I hope you like the traditional Christmas flower."

"I do, and the plant is beautiful." She wrapped her arm around the foil-covered base. A red petal brushed the edge of her cheek. She placed it in the center of the coffee table she'd covered with a red and white runner.

He reached into the bag and handed Sophie a gift wrapped in green tissue paper.

"Mr. Giles!" Her excited daughter sat on the edge of the couch and ripped open the paper. "You got me a shirt for the New England Revolution soccer team. They're my favorite." She turned it around, and her smile got bigger if that was possible. "My name is on the back." She ran over to him and gave him a hug. "This is so great. But it isn't Christmas yet."

"It's a gift from me for helping make Pierre," he said, returning her hug.

Emile came down the stairs. "Hey, Mr. Giles. Thanks for coming to hear us play this evening."

"My pleasure." He handed Emile the second gift from the bag. "I hope you don't have one of these."

"Wow! No, I don't. A light box drawing pad. All these pencils are top-of-the-line. And you got me drawing pads, too!"

Giles took a card from his pocket. "Here's the name of the gallery owner I mentioned, with his cell and email address. I told him about you and sent a photo of Pierre, your snowman. He loved it and would like to talk to you. He'll be away until after New Year's, but he's looking forward to hearing from you."

Emile went to hold out a hand, but he gave Giles a quick hug. “These are the best gifts. Thanks for believing in me.”

Tears filled Elise’s eyes at how her son showed his gratitude. Thoughtful, kind, considerate, generous—the words popped into her head. Her eyes lingered on Giles a little longer. “You didn’t have to give them presents.”

“Consider them thank-you gifts for helping me at the snowman-making contest. The flowers are for my igloo dancing partner.” He grinned and winked.

A blush swept her cheeks. “Give me your coat, and I’ll hang it in the closet. Kids, dinner is ready. Wash your hands, and then we’ll sit down.”

“Mom, please hold on to this card,” Emile said. “I don’t want to lose it.”

The kids headed for the small powder room under the stairs, and she walked into the kitchen. Giles followed.

“Something smells delicious.”

“That’s the Italian bread I just took out of the oven.”

“You look lovely. It’s rare these days for a woman to wear a skirt. Actually, a long skirt is my favorite.”

She’d paired the hunter-green skirt with a cream silk blouse and a fawn-colored leather vest. The gold necklace and teardrop gold earrings had been gifts from her aunt and uncle.

Waves of nervousness quivered in her stomach. The loving banter they'd enjoyed this morning had raised their relationship to a new level. She'd admitted that she was jealous, and he'd said his heart was spoken for. When he put a hand on her shoulder, she stiffened slightly.

"Elise, am I making you uncomfortable?"

She tightly intertwined her fingers and turned about quickly, making the skirt flare out. *Tell him exactly how you feel.*

"When you came through our front door a few weeks ago, you were like a breath of fresh air, filling our lives with nothing but kindness. You're thoughtful, considerate, and generous. You enjoy spending time with my children. In my mind, you're too good to be true…"

He paled slightly and took a step back. "I don't know what to say other than I'm sorry you feel that way. I'll…"

She held out a hand to interrupt him. "I'm not done. I like you—really like you—and you bring out loving emotions I wasn't ready to feel ever again. You know how to show a lady a good time. You're a wonderful dancer and have kissing down pat."

He appeared to relax, and an easy smile filled his face when she stepped into him and slid her arms around his waist. "This happened very quickly, but I'd like to see where this goes between us. Lastly, I'd like one of your direct kisses before the kids come charging into the kitchen."

Chapter 13

Dickens might be a small town, but the citizens knew how to help Giles celebrate the opening of Creperie de Dickens. Yesterday, a line had formed before he'd opened at eleven thirty a.m., and lunchtime had run longer. Elise had made arrangements for the kids to go to Karla's house, so she worked through the dinner hour. Like the night of his open house, they established a routine of preparing and getting the orders out in record time.

Toni and Melanie were true professionals. His new waitstaff greeted customers with smiles, met diners' needs, and answered questions about the food. After closing last evening, the sisters stayed to help clean up and set up the dining room for today.

Lunch was a repeat from yesterday, but at two thirty, he turned the sign on the front door to Closed and walked back into the kitchen. He'd added more chairs to the table to accommodate his new staff, all of whom were enjoying the huge chef salad the sisters had brought for everyone to enjoy.

Toni and Melanie had made quick friends with Elise, for which he was very glad. Until things slowed down, the sisters let him know they'd stay between the lunch and dinner break.

Toni Dwyer had just celebrated her forty-seventh birthday. Her dark brown hair was in short curls, reminding him of Betty Boop. Her thin-framed gold glasses covered her golden-brown eyes. Having dealt with customers at their father's restaurant, she had an inviting personality that made people feel comfortable. She was also the shorter of the two sisters.

Melanie had added blond highlights to her dark brown hair, which she kept in a neat bun at the back of her neck. A feathering of bangs swept her forehead. She was three years younger and a few inches taller than her sister but had the same captivating eye color. Where Toni was more full-figured, Melanie was on the slender side. She had a sweet personality and was a little more reserved.

"Join us," Toni invited Giles. She'd already set out a plate, fork, and napkin. "I tried to change things up since salad is one thing you don't serve."

He grabbed a bottle of water from the refrigerator before joining them at the table. "That's very thoughtful of you." He raised his water in a salute. "It's not champagne, but thanks for making my grand opening go so smoothly. We've only worked together for a day and a half, but I feel like we've been a team much longer."

"Giles, I speak for Melanie, too, but this is the first place we've worked since we sold our father's place. Over the years, we established an efficient working routine, so we didn't know what to expect, considering you were associated with a huge kitchen staff and servers at five-star venues."

Elise raised a questioning eyebrow at Toni's comment, but he quickly said, "As I mentioned the other morning, you have full rein to establish your routine handling the customers out front. I oversee the kitchen. I'm open to any suggestions you have to make things run more smoothly."

"We appreciate that," Melanie added.

His eyes shifted to Elise, and he settled a hand over hers. "Elise saved the day by helping me yesterday until closing."

"Sorry, I can't stay tonight, but your new assistant will be here tomorrow morning."

"I've got a good routine in play. Diners will have to wait a few minutes longer."

"Lyndsay is looking forward to working with a world-class chef."

Giles stiffened at Melanie's words, *world-class chef*. Of course, they knew who he was since they were friends with Lyndsay. An insistent knock on the front door drew their attention.

"Someone doesn't understand the meaning of a Closed sign." He avoided eye contact with Elise and moved away from the table. "Let me send them away."

His hurried footsteps slowed when he saw the face on the other side of the glass front door. No. He didn't need this now, but avoiding her wasn't an option. He turned the lock and opened the door. "We're closed. If you've come for crepes, dinner won't be served for another hour and a half. Maybe I should make the sign twice the size. What are you doing here?"

His former sister-in-law boldly brushed right past him, unwrapped the cashmere scarf around her neck, and turned on him. "You haven't responded to any of my messages, and I was curious to see your little venture."

She'd needed to follow the trendy fashion scene and had added purple streaks to her white hair that brushed her shoulders. She'd always had a heavy hand with makeup. In his opinion, her fake eyelashes were much too long. Her coat brushed the tops of her boots, which weren't designed to be worn in snow.

"We don't have anything to discuss. You got my brother's portion, and I sold my half. It's all yours, just like you always wanted. You now own five-star restaurants."

She ignored his comments and plucked the fingertips of each glove as she slowly removed them. She looked around and sneered. "Small, plain. It reminds me of one of those little creperies you stumble upon off the beaten path in Paris."

"That is exactly the look I was going for."

"You've had plenty of time to get over your self-imposed guilt and accomplish what you came here to do—make amends with the brokenhearted widow and her family. You've done all the prep work. Now, sign the place over to her to make up for the restaurant they couldn't afford. Get back to what you do best—being the spokesman extraordinaire and overseeing the running of five-star restaurants."

Giles shifted a hip and wrapped his arms around his waist. "Carole, you just don't get it! Those restaurants are all yours. You went behind my back and got what you wanted—the property to open another restaurant. When my brother threw that paperwork in my face, I was shocked to see my signature on the purchase documents. My brother told me he was against opening another restaurant. He hired a private security company to do a background check on the couple whom you were bidding against."

"They didn't have enough money, so what did it matter?"

His patience was spent, replaced by seething anger. "What did it matter? You killed their hopes and dreams. Claude Charrette was despondent and died in a car accident, leaving a wife and two children!"

"That had nothing to do with you walking away."

"Did you read the entire investigator's report?"

"No. Why?"

"There was an addendum. Claude was so desperate that he borrowed money from a disreputable lender. They went after the widow for nonpayment. I personally settled the debt."

"I don't see what the problem is. You've settled the debt, so you can come back. I can't run the company alone. I need to concentrate on the new location. The contractors found structural problems, so the blueprints had to be revised to meet building codes. The inspectors are being nitpicky. When finished, this restaurant will outshine all the others."

"As the saying goes, you bit off more than you can chew. Greed and ego make perfect bed partners. Why don't you promote the pastry chef you lured away from me? Did you think I wouldn't find out?"

Her back stiffened, but she remained quiet since she had nothing to say to defend herself.

"We're done. I'm perfectly happy with *my* little creperie and new life in Dickens." He opened the door. "Good luck with your new restaurant."

"You have no idea what you're giving up! I'll be more famous than you and your brother."

"Enjoy your fame and fortune." He locked the door behind her and hurried into the kitchen. He had to speak to Elise. His blood ran cold at the sight of the empty chair. He curled his fingers into fists, not knowing what he was suffering more—anger or frustration. His new employees' eyes were filled with daggers pointed in his direction.

"How much did you hear?"

"Everything! Elise heard that nasty woman's comments. 'Did you make amends with the brokenhearted widow?'" Melanie blasted him. "You purposely opened this restaurant and are signing it over to her to appease your guilty conscience. You're going back to what you do best—running five-star restaurants! She ran out of here in tears!"

Giles gnashed his teeth in anger and pulled his cell phone out of his pocket, hurrying into the vacant dining room. He didn't expect her to answer his call, so he left a message. "Elise, I know you must hate me right now, but I need to talk to you so I can explain what happened. Please call me or text me. Please."

He returned to the kitchen. "She didn't pick up."

"Surprise, surprise. Giles, we can't work for a dishonest, unethical scoundrel," Toni told him. "Lyndsay won't work for you either. You have some explaining to do, or we walk."

He paced, trying to come up with the right explanation. "First of all, I have no plans to give this restaurant to Elise. It's mine, and I'm here to stay. When I was still a major owner of Bascom Restaurant Conglomerate, I had no idea that my former sister-in-law went behind the backs of my brother and me to purchase the property Elise and her husband wanted. She was sneaky and put everything in my name. My brother found out a few months before he passed and accused me of being underhanded."

"Is the property still in your name?" Melanie asked.

"No, I had our lawyers remove my name from everything when I sold Carole my half of the business and paid off the moneylenders so they wouldn't bother Elise."

"So your former sister-in-law was behind all the trouble," Toni confirmed.

"Yes. When my brother passed away, I realized fame, fortune, and killing myself working too many hours weren't worth it."

"How did you wind up in Dickens?" Melanie asked.

"Last year, I visited Axel and Freja Frost and Lars and Jens Jorgensen, who are longtime friends and fell in love with Dickens. I discreetly hired the same security company to find out where Elise had moved to. I was lucky enough to be able to purchase the property next to hers."

"I'm sorry we called you a scoundrel," Toni said. "From all that you have told us, you've been trying to make amends for what your former sister-in-law did to Elise."

"Yes, and I messed up badly. I should have told her who I was right from the beginning, but I went about it ass-backward. I've been trying to show her the real me, who's a nice guy and not the scoundrel who contributed to her husband's death."

"If you had, she probably wouldn't have wanted to have anything to do with you," Toni reasoned.

"You're right, Toni. She's terrific and has made a permanent place in my heart. Her kids, too."

Toni looked at her sister, and she nodded. "Okay, you're really a good guy, so we'll stay."

A small amount of relief filled his body. "Thanks. At least you two are on my side."

"Elise is hurt and wants nothing to do with you. You need to find an opportunity to talk to her alone and explain your side," Melanie encouraged.

He sat in the chair and clasped his hands as if praying. "I need a Christmas miracle."

"Why don't you talk to your friends? Maybe they can help you out."

Giles gave Toni a half smile. "You're thinking a lot more clearly than I am. Thanks for listening and not bailing on me. Things are going to get a lot crazier later with just me making the crepes."

"We'll explain that perfection can't be rushed," Toni said with a little smile.

"I knew I liked you two."

The dinner session was very busy. He somehow got through the evening and didn't mess up any of the orders, but his mind was filled with Elise. She must hate him. He should have been honest with her from the beginning, but he'd made the wrong choices. He sighed with relief when he'd filled the last order.

Toni returned to the kitchen. "Turned the sign on the door and put out the lights. Customer feedback is that they loved the desserts as much as the main dishes."

"At least I did something right."

"We'll start cleaning up. Can't have Lyndsay walk into a dirty kitchen," Melanie added.

"I'd appreciate that. Too bad you can't administer first aid to two broken hearts."

Standing in front of the sink, Toni wrapped a half apron around her waist. "You need an entire first aid kit."

Melanie carried in a stack of tablecloths. "You care very deeply for Elise… Or is it more like love?"

"I've never been in love, so this feeling is unfamiliar to me, but being with her has brought me nothing but happiness. My heart smiles when she's near. She makes me laugh and is caring. We have fun working together, and I love being with her. Thoughts of her fill my head before I fall asleep, and I think about her when I wake up."

Toni slapped him on the back of his shoulder. "You've got it bad. Like that old song, you've got 'Love in the First Degree.'"

His cell rang, and he hoped it was Elise. His elation died, recognizing Axel's number.

"What's going on, or isn't going on, between you and Elise?" His friend's agitated voice filled Giles's ear. "The story I got was Elise called Britta at 2 Sisters and was crying hysterically. Freja and Karla were there and asked what was going on. To encapsulate, you're a lying, backstabbing, no-good scoundrel. You stole her and her husband's dream and broke Elise's heart."

Giles's guilt increased as he heard that Elise had been crying hysterically. "Axel, I swear I didn't do anything dishonest, but I screwed up big-time. I need to apologize to Elise, but she doesn't want to have anything to do with me."

"You mean you need to eat an entire humble pie. I've choked on it a few times. When are you finished for the evening?"

"I'll be leaving the creperie in half an hour."

"Come to my house. Freja should be finished getting the girls settled in bed by then."

"Are you sure she'll let me in the door?"

"Haha. We'll figure something out. See you in a few."

"Thanks, Axel."

Toni and Melanie finished cleaning up the kitchen. "Thanks for all of your help. I'm on my way to talk to Axel and Freja."

"We'll lock up. See you in the morning, boss."

Fifteen minutes later, Giles knocked on his friend's front door. Freja greeted him, unsmiling, but held up an aluminum pie plate with a pie server. "I hope you brought your appetite."

Axel was holding a bottle of Tums.

"Very funny, you two."

They sat at the kitchen table, and Freja poured them cups of coffee. "Since I almost lost Axel due to miscommunication, I learned to take a step back, not jump to conclusions and hear both sides."

"Fair enough, and thanks for listening."

Giles started with Carole DeLuc showing up at the restaurant and explaining what his former sister-in-law had done to ensure Elise didn't get the property for her and her husband's restaurant and then put everything in his name. He told them about his brother's poor health and passing, which had triggered Giles to give up his corporate life. He also included what he knew about Elise's late husband's financial troubles and paying off the loan.

"Where would Elise get the idea that you purchased the property away from them and felt guilty enough to start a restaurant and give it to her before you returned to Chicago?" Freja asked.

"Elise ran out before I put Carole in her place, so everything she's thinking is wrong. I called her, but she wants nothing to do with me." He hung his head. "I feel sick over this whole situation. I should have told her my reason for coming here from the start. Poor choice."

"We know about poor choices. Ours lasted twenty years-plus," Axel explained, turning his head and giving his wife's hand a loving squeeze.

"I'm sorry this is happening to you. Are you in love with Elise?" Freja asked.

"Toni and Melanie, my terrific new waitstaff, asked me the same thing. It happened very quickly, so I'm still a little love shell-shocked."

"I like that, love shell-shocked. We need to get you two together in a place she won't suspect is a setup," Axel suggested.

"I can't take any time off from work. Lyndsay Barnes, my new assistant, starts tomorrow and will be learning the routine."

Freja's eyes opened in surprise. "I met Lyndsay Barnes when I went to culinary school in New York. She studied in Pais but was leaning toward a dietitian degree. A pretty woman with blond hair."

"That's her. Stop in the creperie tomorrow. I'm sure she'll be glad to see you after all these years."

"I will, but back to setting up a makeup rendezvous."

Freja pulled out her cell phone and called up her calendar. "The one place she won't find suspicious is the event center. I know she'll be there tomorrow evening for the dress rehearsal for *The Bells of St. Dickens*. This year, live music will precede and follow the play, so Sebastian will be there with the band kids."

"We're surprising the kids with a holiday disco party with refreshments after rehearsal as a thank-you for all their hard work," Axel said. "I can arrange for the depot alarm to go off, and Elise will want to check it out. I'll text you just before I test the system to give you a heads-up. I'll unlock the door so you can get in."

"I can be at the depot by eight-thirty p.m. I hope she'll believe me." Giles felt a little better and finished his coffee.

Axel slipped his arm around Freja's waist and pulled her close. "True love doesn't run smoothly. We've survived many bumps, but each one brought us a little closer, strengthening our love."

"I should be so lucky. Thanks for your help."

Twenty minutes later, he pulled into his driveway and hesitated to get out of the car. Elise's house was dark except for the tree lights shining in the front window. One minute, things had been wonderful between them, and now everything he'd wanted to prevent was biting him in the butt. The urge was strong to go over there, but he anticipated that voices raised in anger would surely upset the kids. Hopefully, he and Elise could work things out tomorrow night.

He let himself into the house and didn't bother to turn on the tree lights. Not even their beauty could pull him out of the doldrums. He wanted to take a shower but needed to check his email. He'd placed a special order for imported chocolate and wanted to see if the company had sent him a shipping date.

He opened his laptop and reviewed his few messages. There wasn't a message from the company, but the one from the County Historical Society was a surprise and most welcome. When he'd done his initial research, he'd joined the organization. Sharing his email had been required. He'd asked if there was any additional information on the old depot in Dickens and Ringing Rocks House.

The message was from the vice president of the organization, who just happened to be the great-great-great-grandson of the sheriff who'd raided the brothel. Their relatives had shared their old records with the Historical Society. Ringing Rocks House had belonged to Bessie Doyle, a madam of the brothel and a gambler. She'd also overseen the "parlor" at the Dickens Depot, where she'd provided tea for the ladies and hard liquor for the gentlemen. Card games, which hadn't exactly been legal, had been available. When the gentlemen had had too much to drink, she'd invite them to the brothel for female companionship, who would relieve the men of their watches and money.

"Doyle! That's why Thaddeus and Tillie *Doyle* hate the depot and never recognize the historical status of Elise's house." He continued reading.

After numerous complaints, the sheriff raided the depot and house of ill repute. Bessie was arrested and sent to jail for six months. The gamblers escaped without prosecution. The sheriff and his brother took over the hotel and renamed it Dickens Lodging.

They were getting closer. Even though it was after ten o'clock, he replied to the email, thanking him for the information and asking if there were additional photos of the hotel's ledgers that might be more legible.

A few minutes later, he got a response email with six photos attached. A smile slowly filled his face. *C. Dickens* was on three pages. The dates and place were right, but had this *really* been Charles Dickens?

At least Giles wouldn't go into his meeting with Elise empty-handed.

Friday evening, Elise stood back and admired the disco ball Shawn had just finished hanging in the center of the music room. "Thanks for helping decorate at the last minute, but we wanted to surprise the kids."

The stage manager folded the stepladder and chuckled. "This is the room where the band kids practice and have music lessons, so a disco ball fits right in."

"Make sure you join us after the show. We're having pizza delivered."

"I will. Now I'm off to work the lights for rehearsal."

Elise finished setting out the cupcakes and cookies the kids would enjoy at their surprise holiday party. Freja and Karla set the coolers, already filled with drinks, under the long tables where they'd also set out snack bags of treats.

It had taken every bit of acting ability to put up a good front, especially for her children. Inside, Elise felt betrayed and sick at heart. It was happening all over again, the same feeling she'd suffered when she'd learned Claude had lost their money and gotten a loan from crooked moneylenders.

What a fool she'd been, falling for Giles's smooth, slick line. He'd worked his way into her children's hearts, too. Even Simone was fooled by him. Was she so desperate for male companionship, someone who was kind, thoughtful, loving… Her inner instinct had been right on target. Giles DeLuc had been too good to be true.

Don't think about him now. They'd planned a fun night for the children.

Freja hurried in, carrying a tray filled with cellophane bags. "Britta just dropped these off. Fudge goodies for each of the kids to take home."

"Has rehearsal started? Sophie is nervous and excited. She doesn't want me to watch her until opening night."

"Holly and Ivy are excited, too. Sebastian is directing the kids to play the opening songs. Axel is up in the booth with Shawn, controlling the lights. I'm helping Karla keep the kids in line, so they go onstage at the right time."

"Everything is set here." Elise's phone vibrated in her pocket, and she frowned at the alert. "Something just triggered the alarm at the depot."

"Do you want me to notify the others?" Freja asked.

"No. They're getting the same message but probably have their phones silenced. I'm sure it's a mistake. I'll clear it with the security company, but I'll go over and check out the building."

"I'll let the others know you're taking care of it, but be careful."

Her first thought was someone was out to sabotage the light show again, which didn't make sense since the lights weren't connected to the building.

She hurried into her office to get her coat and hat but remembered to bring a flashlight. The night air was bitterly cold, and her breath misted when she hurried up the hill. She started walking faster when she saw that the lights were on inside the building.

She reasoned that a burglar wouldn't have turned the lights on, and there wasn't anything to steal anyway. She stepped up onto the platform and turned the doorknob. The intruder had turned on the propane stove, so the interior was warm. Looking around, she noticed that the door to the future museum was open, and the lights were on in there, too.

Her heart pounded. Coming here alone hadn't been such a good idea. She took out her cell phone and typed in a message to Axel. He was a lot closer than the police. *Burglar in the depot. I need help.* But she hesitated before pushing send. Taking a deep breath, she stepped into the room. Her fear subsided, but her heart continued to beat fast and furious.

A small folding table and two chairs had been brought in. Giles sat in one, unsmiling. He leaned forward on his elbows, but his hands were fisted together in a tightened grip.

She shoved her phone in her pocket and wrapped her arms around her waist. "So this was a setup."

"Yes. I was desperate to get you alone so I could explain."

Elise took a couple of steps closer, yanked off her hat, and shoved it in her coat pocket. He wanted to tell her his side, but she was going to have her say first!

"You want to explain to appease your guilty conscience, but not before I have my say! Giles DeLuc, you're a phony! A low-life reprobate! You played me and used my kids and the cat! You're the mega owner of Bascom Restaurant Conglomerate! Five restaurants weren't enough! To think I poured my heart out to you about Claude being swindled, and you already knew! Now I've got spine-crackers after me!"

Spent, she felt warm tears run down her cheeks, but she didn't bother to wipe them away. "I feel like a dupe! My husband deceived me, and you lied to me, too!"

She thrust an arm in the direction of the event center. "My children think you're wonderful and caring. How do I tell them you aren't what you've led them to believe? You're a lying, rotten snake in the grass."

She took a deep breath. "You want to appease your guilty conscience by signing over the restaurant to me? Don't bother. I wouldn't accept it if it came with a million dollars! Go back to Chicago and plan your new fancy restaurant opening."

She'd let him have it, big-time. He winced when she accused him of using her children but remained surprisingly quiet during her tirade. Did she really want to hear what he had to say? Did he deserve a chance to defend himself? He could have walked away, but he'd cared enough to set up this time alone with her. "I'm done."

"If I'd been honest with you from the beginning, all of this torment and misunderstanding could have been avoided."

She opened the zipper of her jacket and sat on the edge of the chair. "On that, I'll agree. Continue."

He leaned against the back of the chair. "I'm the *former* owner of those five restaurants—meaning I'm no longer associated with Bascom. My *former* sister-in-law bid on the property but put everything in my name. I didn't find out what she'd done until my brother brought it to my attention."

"So you had no idea your sister-in-law planned to open another restaurant?"

"No. Both my brother and I were against opening another location. I was so consumed with making a name for myself that I neglected my dying brother. When I realized fame and fortune weren't all they were cracked up to be, I sold her my half of the business before moving to Dickens."

Now, she felt lower than low and shook her head. "So your sister-in-law is the one I should be telling off."

"Too late. She's gone back to Chicago to concentrate on opening another restaurant. She's got problems but won't be getting any help from me." He took one of her hands and squeezed it a little. "The spine-crackers won't be coming after you. I paid them in full."

Her eyes flared wide, but she didn't pull her hand away. "You really must enjoy taking me by surprise. Giles, that was a lot of money."

"I still have a lot of money, but it doesn't matter. If my former sister-in-law hadn't raised the stakes, your husband wouldn't have tried to get more money to purchase the building."

She recognized he was carrying around a lot of guilt for something he hadn't done. Her instincts had been right all along. He was wonderful, thoughtful, and honorable. "All this time, you've been doing these wonderful things for us to make amends for something that wasn't your fault."

He shrugged. "You could put it that way, but nothing was forced. Everything I did was genuinely given from my heart. Had I told you right from the start who I was, would you have had anything to do with me?"

"Probably not, but your strategy worked. Knowing the goodness and kindness in your heart, I understand where you're coming from."

"I'm really sorry you lost your dream of opening your own place, resulting in Claude's death. I would have stopped her if I had known what she was doing."

"I believe you."

As far as she was concerned, he'd beaten himself up enough. Elise removed her coat and made herself comfortable on his lap. She ran a slow hand down his cheek. "I'm sorry for all the nasty things I said to you. Feeling guilty ends now. No more beating yourself up for something you didn't do. It's time to start healing."

He took her hand and kissed the center of her palm. "So that you understand, I didn't do those things for you and the kids to make amends. You, Emile, and Sophie have brought so much love and happiness into my life. I did them because I wanted to."

She leaned in and kissed the tip of his nose. "Love?"

"You caught that word, did you?" He grinned. "We just met, and people will argue that love doesn't happen so quickly." He placed her hand on the center of his chest. "My heart is overflowing with love for you and those two imps. I'm not expecting miracles, but however long it takes, I want you, Emile, and Sophie, to become a permanent part of my life."

A film of happy tears coated her eyes and started running down her cheeks. "I've said it before, and I don't think I'll ever stop saying it. You're too good to be true. You've worked your way into my heart, too. As for us becoming a permanent part of your life, miracles do happen."

He laughed out loud and pulled her closer. "You didn't say no."

Their mouths met in a long, sweet kiss, and she snuggled her head on his shoulder. He tightened his arms around her waist.

"When do you have to get back to the kids?" he asked, running his hand up and down her back.

"About a half hour."

The wall where the contractors had revealed more of the tiles surrounding the fireplace drew her attention. "After the holidays, I have to research this place in-depth. I want to prove the depot's historical value. It will be like putting duct tape over the mouths of those nonbelievers. We still need to find out who disconnected the power sources from the lights display."

"I have a gift for you."

"Enough." *Kiss.* "With." *Kiss.* "The." *Kiss.* "Gifts." *Kiss.* "You don't have to prove anything to me."

"Thanks for all the kisses. I'd get up, but I like having you on my lap. Reach under my chair for my laptop and set it on the table. Get ready for your questions to be answered. The vice president of the County Historical Society reached out to me with answers to the questions I had about the depot and your house."

Elise read through all the information and was amazed by what had been provided. "Thaddeus Doyle was related to a madam who ran a brothel and a gambler. No wonder he wanted to keep everything a secret."

"I'll bet he's the one who tampered with the holiday lights, too."

"It makes me a little sad knowing this room was once used for activities outside the law."

"Now, don't hit me, but your house was once a brothel," he reminded her.

She slapped him playfully on the chest anyway. "At least I'm not related to a madam!"

"It isn't all bad. They served tea to the ladies while they waited for the train."

"There is that. The sheriff and his brother purchased my house." She read a little more, and her excitement amped up. "According to these hotel registers, C. Dickens slept at Ringing Rocks."

"I researched when Charles Dickens visited this area, so it's possible."

Elise shifted on Giles's lap. "I keep forgetting to look at the pictures we found in my house. We can hang them here if they're from the right time period. We'll focus more on it being a depot rather than a gambling venue. Thaddeus and Tillie are going to be embarrassed, but we'll focus on the author's visit."

"We need to put this argument to rest. I think the Dickens Historical Society should have an emergency meeting on Sunday evening right here in this room. We'll show the county information and stress that Charles Dickens came through this depot and stayed at Ringing Rocks. Now, are we good?"

"We're perfect." She stood and wiggled her hips. "I hope you have your dancing shoes on."

"Why?

"After rehearsal, we're having a surprise party for the kids, complete with a disco ball in the center of the music rehearsal room. Shawn will be the DJ."

Giles slipped his arms around her and twirled her around. "I have the perfect song, but I don't think the kids will appreciate a slow dance."

"What song did you want him to play?"

He rolled his forehead over hers. "'When a Man Loves A Woman,' Home Free's version."

"I love that version, too. How about we save it for a dance in the igloo?"

"You're on," he agreed.

She swung him around one more time. "Do you remember the excitement you felt as a child when you woke up Christmas morning, seeing all the gifts Santa had left?"

"It's been a long time, but I can remember that special kind of happiness."

"That's what I'm feeling right now. Giles, I haven't felt like this in a very long time. Let's party!"

Chapter 14

Saturday evening, Giles presented the second Cocoa Crawl gift basket to the winner at the end of a very busy day. The couple had just finished eating their dinner at the creperie.

Once again, he'd had a line waiting to get in for lunch and dinner. Toni and Melanie had handled the crowd with ease. His new hires were more than he could have ever wished for. Lyndsay knew her stuff, and they worked well together.

He'd visited the shops when the creperie was closed, and the feedback had been more positive than last week. Word had spread about the small community's fun event, drawing more visitors. This was the last Saturday before Christmas when everyone decided to do or finish their holiday shopping.

Traffic was still heavy when he left the shop and headed for the final night of the Dickens Holiday of Lights show. He'd spoken to Elise a little while ago, and she had told him that tourists had come to see the lights even though they didn't have a reservation.

Things between them were perfect. The holiday disco party was a lot of fun. They'd entered the party room to see Shawn turning on the colorful revolving light and playing the first song, "Celebration" by Kool and the Gang.

The kids had run in and started dancing. He'd never been a "dancer of disco," but he'd joined in the fun with his friends. The parents had arrived a little early, and they, too, had gotten "into the groove."

He found a parking spot and walked up the hill to the depot. Visitors were milling around, some drinking hot chocolate. When he stepped inside, all the benches were filled. He saw Elise behind the refreshment stand, restacking the cups used for hot chocolate. She hurried over.

"This is absolutely nuts! Next year, we'll run the event four weekends, the first one the weekend following Thanksgiving. It's only eight thirty p.m. Did you close the creperie early?"

"Lyndsay assured me she could handle the last few orders. Toni and Melanie said they'd clean up. I'm giving them all a raise."

"I'm so happy you have a great assistant."

"So you're no longer jealous?" he teased.

"Nope!" Her smile faded. "Karla notified everyone of tomorrow night's special meeting. She told me that certain members protested, but she insisted they be present. The meeting wouldn't be long, but there was an important presentation that they shouldn't miss."

"You're being very kind, not focusing on the darker side the depot was used for, saving the Doyles from embarrassment."

"They'll be shocked enough when we show them the pictures." She checked the time on the big schoolhouse clock. "The last visitor train will leave in five minutes. Then it's our turn. My aunt and uncle just pulled into the parking lot."

Giles adjusted the conductor's cap he'd put on before getting out of the car.

"All aboard!"

Sunday evening, Giles looked around the soon-to-be Dickens Depot Museum. After what they planned to reveal this evening, there shouldn't be any doubt about the historical status of the building and Ringing Rocks House.

This afternoon, they brought in two portable heaters and two dozen chairs. They also hung a number of photos for tonight's presentation. Elise decided this wasn't a social gathering that included refreshments.

When he'd stopped at the diner for coffee and a breakfast sandwich, he'd asked Amy Doritt if there had been any gossip about tonight's meeting. She'd leaned into the counter, attempting to keep their conversation quiet. The three couples had had breakfast together but had been unusually quiet.

Of course, she'd asked what this meeting was all about. His only comeback had been that the question of the depot's historical designation would be settled. He hadn't waited around for her to ask any other questions.

A shroud of doom and gloom followed the members when they arrived—the three biddies and their husbands and the Doritts. Tom Gridley sat next to Amy. Jillian Morgan, Matt Mathews and Trix Warden all sat together.

Shawn accompanied his Aunt Matilda. He wasn't surprised when the mayor walked in. Although she wasn't a member of the Historical Society, Karla, as the president, had let her know this presentation would be of great importance to the citizens of Dickens. Madeline St. Vincent, the editor-in-chief of the *Dickens Gazette*, was the last one to hurry in. Sebastian and Axel didn't bother to sit but stood next to Giles for moral support.

Karla opened the meeting. "Thank you for attending this special meeting. Over the past couple of years, the historical designation of the train tracks and the depot has been highly debated. Thanks to Elise and Giles, the debate can now be put to rest. I'll turn the meeting over to Elise."

Giles gave her a thumbs-up when she stood at the front of the room. "With the help of the County Historical Society's vice president, we've uncovered information about the depot. If you doubt my information, you can contact that organization."

She ran her finger along the beautiful blue and white tiles. “This room was once a parlor where travelers waited between trains. Tea and hard liquor were served. Card games were available to those who wanted to indulge. Unfortunately, gamblers fleeced travelers. Once they were inebriated, they were lured to a local brothel, where they were entertained.” She hesitated but then continued. “That brothel was…Ringing Rocks House. As you all know, that’s my house.”

Giles studied the faces of Tillie and Thaddeus Doyle. Both had lowered their heads, anticipating being embarrassed.

“After quite a number of complaints, the sheriff raided the depot and the brothel. The owner was arrested and jailed for six months. Subsequently, the sheriff and his brother purchased the brothel and turned it into Dickens Lodging.”

“Was he able to provide the name of the owner?” Thaddeus Doyle asked.

“It’s not important,” she replied in a nonchalant voice. “The best historical proof is who visited the depot and stayed at my house.” Elise nodded to Giles. “Please remove the covering from the first photo. These were found in the attic of my house.”

Giles removed the white sheet from the photo they’d hung on the wall earlier.

“This black-and-white picture is of the depot,” Elise noted. “As you can see, the period of dress is approximately the mid to late 1800s.”

Giles removed the next drape and addressed the audience. “This one was taken of the depot’s interior. Note the ticket booth is the original.”

He removed the drapes from the other pictures, including one of a steam locomotive waiting for passengers.

“Axel found old photos in the former milk room just off the area where the train club is set up,” Elise continued. “The construction materials for the bank barn were transported by rail car. Another photo shows the partial framework of the barn. There is a stone marker with the year 1840.”

Murmurings started among the members, and Giles nodded at Elise to pass around the photocopies they had made of the guest ledgers from Dickens Lodging.

“The county posted a faded hotel register, but the script is hard to read,” she explained. “One looks like C. Dickens. There’s a partial, very faded date of 1867. Dickens traveled through this area by rail on his way to Boson in 1867, his second visit to the US. His first visit was in 1842, and he also traveled through this area.

“As you can see, there is a great deal of history in the depot and my house, not that I’m proud it was once a brothel,” Elise added with a little laugh.

Karla moved to stand next to Elise. “Thank you, Elise and Giles, for this wonderful presentation. I believe we have solid proof of the Dickens Depot’s historical designation. I propose that over the next year, while repairs are being made, we plan the interior of our museum. All in favor, raise their hand."

All hands were raised.

Giles felt the pressure of Axel's hand on his shoulder. "Thanks for going the extra mile to prove the historical value of this place. You're a true friend."

The sincerity of his longtime friend was much appreciated. "My pleasure. That's what friends are for."

Elise moved to stand beside him. They were a couple, and he wanted to shout it from the rooftops but settled for securing her hand in his. He wasn't surprised when Tillie and Thaddeus approached them. The other members were studying the photographs.

"You know the name of the person who owned the brothel. Why did you remain silent?" Thaddeus asked.

"Would you have preferred we embarrass you?" Giles asked.

"Of course not!" He guffawed.

"That's why we didn't mention your name," Elise explained. "We understand why you've remained silent about your family's colorful background for fear of embarrassment. I'm just curious. Do you know what happened to Bessie when she got out of jail?"

Tillie Doyle laughed. "Oh, she moved to Philadelphia and started a finishing school for young ladies."

"Now that's what I call a career change," Giles said, fighting hard not to burst out laughing.

"Thank you both," Tillie said. "This is the best Christmas present we've ever been given."

"We're also sorry for trying to ruin your light show last week. Come on, Tillie, let's look at the pictures."

"Well, you did it!" Karla gave them each a quick hug. "I don't think we'll have trouble with the gossip queens. They're all enthused about setting up the museum and even have pieces of period furniture they'd like to donate."

Sebastian slipped his arm around his wife's waist. "Thanks for making this happen. It's time to head home. We'll see you at the play tomorrow night, which is Christmas Eve."

Elise wanted to make this Christmas perfect for her children, and it turned out better than she could have imagined. At seven Christmas morning, Giles knocked at her door, bringing crepes and gifts. He placed them under the tree, and then she rang a string of authentic sleigh bells she'd found in the attic. The kids came running down the stairs and started opening their gifts.

When Sophie opened Giles's gift, she jumped up and down. It was tickets to see the New England Revolution soccer team. Four tickets were included so they could all attend. His other gift was a jewelry-making craft set. She planned to make a bracelet for each of her friends, spelling out their names.

Emile's gift was a certificate for an online graphics course. The gallery owner was also a professor and would work directly with Emile. His other gift was a pair of ice skates.

Giles was overwhelmed when Emile presented a framed picture of Emile's licorice candy character. The red, skinny, piano-key character had six extra arms and wore a chef's hat. Giles was going to hang it in the dining room at the creperie. Everyone laughed when he opened the box that contained a bird feeder and a bag of bird feed.

He apologized to Elise. Although there wasn't a box big enough to hold her present, he told her he would give it to her this evening.

Elise sensed something was up because the kids giggled.

After breakfast, Giles accompanied them to church. He told her that he hadn't attended Christmas Day services in quite a while. She also found out that he had a very nice singing voice.

They'd all been invited to dinner at Karla and Sebastian's house. Elise's aunt and uncle were also invited. Once again, they made room for everyone to enjoy celebrating together, adding an additional long table to the family room.

After a dinner of honey-glazed ham and all the trimmings, organized chaos ensued when the kids started opening more gifts. Elise laughed at the pile of wrappings, thinking about all the time it had taken to wrap the gifts.

After a dessert of Bûche de Noël and special holiday crepes with ice cream, the kids scattered, and Karla took the baby upstairs for a nap. Elise's aunt, uncle, Lars and Jens were watching Irving Berlin's *White Christmas* in the family room. She and Freja volunteered to put away the leftovers. They were just about finished when Giles came into the kitchen, wearing his coat and hat.

He held out her coat. "Time to get your Christmas present."

Freja, Sebastian, and Axel were standing in the doorway. All were grinning.

"From those grins, you all know what my gift is," Elise said, zipping up the front of her puffy coat.

"Have fun. We've got the kids," Freja assured with a big smile.

The car was already warm when they pulled away from the house. "Where are we going?"

"Home," he said, keeping his eyes on the road.

"Ah, we left the children and a ton of gifts."

"Trust me."

She had no idea what he was doing but decided to enjoy this private time with the man who filled her heart with joy. She was further confused when he pulled into her driveway. She didn't bother to ask questions since she already knew he wouldn't answer.

He reached into the back of the car for a gift bag. "Present time. We'll be outside, so wear your hat and gloves."

He put a hand on her elbow and guided her along the side of the house to the back, where she was greeted by a spotlight that illuminated the rocks.

"What's all this?"

"Your Christmas present." He guided her to stand a foot away from the rocks before reaching into the bag. He pulled out a ball-peen hammer and a white file card with numbers.

"I didn't give Sebastian much time, but he did the best he could. He got a specific tone from each rock to make up a little song. The number on each rock is written in playing order."

She leaned back slightly, shocked, surprised, overwhelmed. "This is my Christmas present? You had him write a song according to the rocks?" She couldn't stop smiling. This was unbelievable!

He bent slightly and presented her with the small hammer. "Do you need me to hold out the card?"

"No," she said with a chuckle. She studied the numbers on the card and located them close together on the rocks. "Let me do a test." The first tap created a reverberating sound that was quite pleasant. The hammer pulsed slightly in her hand. "My house is really musical!" She stepped a little closer. "Okay, I can do this."

"I'm recording your first concert. Presenting Elise Charrette in her debut performance. Go."

She went through the song once, twice, and by the third time, she added the words to a familiar song. "I love you a bushel and a peck, a bushel and a peck and a hug around the neck."

Giles clapped when she finished. Tears ran down her cheeks. She threw her arms around his neck and pecked him on the cheek. "You knew what I was going to play."

"Yes. Sebastian thought I had lost it completely. There's nothing like the rocks sending you a message about how I feel about you."

She put a hand to the back of her ear, pretending to catch a sound. "Did you hear that?"

"What?" he asked in all seriousness, looking around.

"The rocks echoed, sending you a message. I love you, too."

"Too bad we can't get the rocks to play 'Hallelujah.'" He slipped an arm around her waist. "It's cold. Let's go back to the car. I do have one other gift for you." He pushed a button on his phone, and the lights went out.

She leaned back against the warm seat cushion, turned, and smiled at him. "This has been the best Christmas ever, and I don't need another gift."

This time, her gift was in a long, narrow box. She removed the ribbon and the lid. Inside was a travel brochure for France.

"Are you kidding me?" She could barely get the words out from the tightness in her throat.

He shifted so that he could face her and took her hand. "Next summer, we'll go to France. Emile can visit the museums he's dreamed of visiting. We'll explore small creperies that offer the best crepes. We can go to Marseille to get madeleines. We'll take Sophie to a professional football, aka soccer, game. What do you say?"

She glanced at the brochure one more time. Her mind and heart were in total agreement. "I'll go on only one condition. We go as a family."

"I guess what they say is true. Christmas is the season for miracles."

"Giles, you're *my* miracle. Merry Christmas."

Author's Note

I hope you enjoyed your visit to Dickens. I have two other books in the series, and you met the characters in this book.

Karla and Sebastian's book is "The Bells of St. Dickens." Freja and Axel's story is "Kringle All the Way."

I hope you'll read all of the other wonderful books in the Dickens series.

After reading "Dicken's Holiday of Lights," please take a few minutes to leave a review.

Also, visit my website to sign up for my newsletter to stay up to date on what's happening in my writing world.

Happy Reading!

Judy

Website: http://www.judykentrus.com

Facebook: https://www.facebook.com/judykentrusauthor/

Instagram: https://www.instagram.com/judykentrus/?hl=en

Bookbub: https://www.bookbub.com/profile/judy-kentrus

Other Great Reads by

Judy Kentrus

BEACON POINTE BOOKS

Romantic Suspense

THE ASSOCIATION

Stand-alone Books

ELUSIVE OBSESSION

MAID TO ORDER

UNSUNG HERO

BLUEBERRY TWIST

Sweet Romance

GUY

Last Man Standing

AURORA

Always a Bridesmaid

THE BELLS OF ST. DICKENS

Dickens Holiday Romance

KRINGLE ALL THE WAY

Dickens Holiday Romance

DICKENS HOLIDAY OF LIGHTS

Dickens Holiday Romance

WHERE DREAMS COME TRUE

Last Chance Beach Romance

BEACON OF THANKS

Last Chance Beach Romance

LAUREL HEIGHTS BOOKS

ARREST OF THE HEART

Book 1

WINNER TAKES ALL - (Part One)

Book 2

THE WEDDING GIFT - (Part Two)

Book 3

TEA IN TIME

Book 4

FROZEN HEARTS

Book 5

US PARK RANGER SERIES

A KISS AT SUNSET

Book 1

KISS OF FIRE

Book 2

A TIMELESS KISS

Book 3

HISTORICAL ROMANTIC SUSPENSE

Spirit of the Winds

Check out my website for the link to download the

FREE prequel to Spirit of the Winds.

COMING MARCH 2025

Spirit of the Seas

EDEN PRAIRIE HOLIDAY SERIES

DANIELLE'S CHRISTMAS WISH

Plus

Danielle's Snowy Wish

Bonus Short Story

Book 1

WRONG TURN, RIGHT HEART

Book 2

A Valentine's Day Romance

A WITCH'S TALE

Book 3

ANOTHER NEW YEAR'S EVE

Book 4

<u>TASTE OF SUMMER</u>

Book 5

<u>DANIEL'S TICKET TO HEAVEN</u>

Book 6

Vanderbilt Series

LOVE NEVER DIES

Book 1

Billionaire FOR SALE

Book 2

SONG OF MY HEART

Book 3